HOLIDAY HORROR . . .

Merely Hall was famous for producing the finest tapestries in England. People came from everywhere to see them. But on Christmas morning all eyes were glued to the body of the young American in the front hallway. The local constable called it an accident, but Inspector Gently had other suspicions. He knew that anyone—the wealthy widow, the brilliant weaver, the jealous Welshman, the flirtatious maid, and even the impeccable lord of the manor—could be the culprit. He was determined to unravel the sinister design behind this masterpiece of murder.

D0035355

Scene Of The Crime ® Mysteries

Murder Ink.® Mysteries

A Scene Of The Crime® Mystery

LANDED GENTLY

Alan Hunter

A DELL BOOK

Published by
Dell Publishing Co., Inc.
1 Dag Hammarskjold Plaza
New York, New York 10017

LANDED GENTLY was originally published by
Cassell & Company, Ltd., London.

TO MY WIFE

who never fails to listen respectfully when I read
to her what comes out of my typewriter, nor ever
fails to criticize it justly, fearlessly, and with an
almost prophetic insight,

THIS BOOK

Dell ® TM 681510, Dell Publishing Co., Inc.

ISBN: 0-440-14711-5

Reprinted by arrangement with
Macmillan Publishing Co., Inc.

Printed in the United States of America

First Dell printing—February 1982

EDUCATIONAL NOTE

Those readers familiar with the glories of Holkham will be in no doubt as to the source of a number of architectural details distributed about this novel. Those who are not so familiar are recommended to close the book immediately and to hasten to repair an education gravely defective. It should not be necessary to add, but I do so out of courtesy, that the characters in the book, unlike the architecture, are wholly fictitious, and have existed nowhere except in the mind of

Sincerely yours,
ALAN HUNTER

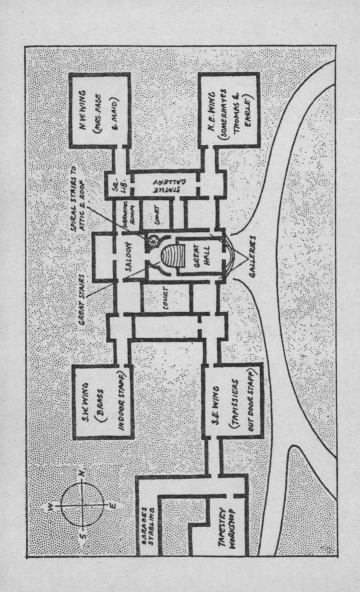

CHAPTER ONE

'COME IN, Dutt.'

'Yessir. Thank you, sir.'

'Grab yourself one of Mrs. Jarvis's mince-pies and have a warm by the fire.'

'Don't mind if I do, sir. It's perishing cold enough for brass monkeys outside.'

Gratefully the Cockney Sergeant tugged off his gauntlets and spread his numbed hands before the blaze. There was always a good fire in Gently's room, he remembered, his senior had picked himself a jewel among landladies. It wasn't all bunce, being a family man. . . .

Down below the frosty dusk of a December afternoon was settling in the quiet Finchley road. Opposite Gently's rooms the trees of a public garden made a gloomy and forbidding mass, and the street-lights, old-fashioned and inadequate, seemed to withdraw inside their tear-shaped globes. Another dose of fog on the way, no doubt. Up here you didn't notice it so much, but as soon as you got down to St. John's Wood or a bit further in that direction. . . . Dutt shivered and sank his teeth into one of the still hot mince-pies.

'These is a bit of all right, sir!' he mumbled crumbily.

His chief grinned at him over the expensive new pike-rod he was playing with. 'They're laced with brandy, Dutt . . . it's Mrs. Jarvis's special recipe. And talking of brandy, how about a drop of something?'

'Yessir—you bet.'

'Whisky would you like?'

'Same as you, sir.'

Gently put down the rod with care and went over to the tray on his sideboard. Strange it was going to be, spending Christmas away from his familiar and comfortable rooms. Here were his usual collection of bottles, beside them a lavish bowl of fruit and a dish of nuts; holly garnished the photographs of his police college days, the case of his twenty-six-pound pike, the top of the bookcase with its rows of Notable British Trials and angling classics. And in the deep, generous Edwardian fireplace, magnificently wasteful, burned the sort of fire that Mrs. Jarvis knew he liked, casting its flickering glow on the copper coal-scuttle. Twenty . . . no, twenty-one Christmases he had spent in this room, with Dutt and the others dropping in, sometimes bringing their families. . . .

'Cheers, Dutt.'

'All the best, sir.'

'Let's hope it's a quiet Christmas.'

'Would make a change, sir, wouldn't it?'

Gently picked up the rod again and swished it once or twice experimentally. A real beauty, that. It must have cost his colleagues over a tenner. And his name on it, too, engraved on a little oval silver plate let into the butt.

'Anyway, they won't be calling me out! That's one consolation.'

'No, sir. You're fireproof this time. They can't call out the guest of a flipping Chief Constable.'

'And it's a long way away, up there in North Northshire. I shan't look at a paper, Dutt, all the time I'm away.'

'Don't blame you either, sir. Shut the hangar door is what I says.'

Gently sighed softly and delicately dismantled the rod. He had to keep on telling himself that he liked the idea of being out of London for Christmas. Out of the blue it had come, that invitation. Two mornings ago he'd found a memo on his desk saying that the Assistant Commissioner wanted to see him.

'Didn't know you were a pal of Sir Daynes Broke, Gently.'

'Sir Daynes Broke . . . ?' Gently had stared at him.

'He's been on the phone about that escaped convict, and asked if you were getting a break over Christmas. I said yes, probably, and he asked if you'd be interested in some good pike-fishing. You are, aren't you?'

'Yes . . . of course.'

'That's what I told him. And he came up with an invitation for you to spend Christmas with him. I must say some of you blokes don't waste your time when you're out in the country.'

They'd all envied him, of course. They'd been collecting several weeks to make him a present to commemorate his twenty years with the Central Office, and a pike-rod was just the thing. But Gently himself wasn't so sure of his good fortune. After twenty-one Christmases spent with Mrs. Jarvis, he'd got into a pleasant rut, a rut that just suited him. . . .

And all he knew of Sir Daynes, anyway, was what he had seen of him when he'd been out on a case.

'That's a good drop of Scotch, sir!' Dutt was smacking his lips appreciatively.

'Have another one, Dutt.'

'No, sir. Not if you don't mind.'

'I suppose I'd better be getting my traps together. That train goes in an hour. And if I know Liverpool Street two days before Christmas. . . .'

Dutt fumbled in the pocket of his overcoat and produced a small package done up in Christmas wrapping-paper.

'Here, sir. From the Missus and me and the kids.'

Gently untied a wealth of tinselled tape to reveal a pretty little sand-blasted briar, almost an exact replica of the one Dutt had seen in his chief's mouth so often.

'If you don't like it, sir, they says they'll change it, but I reckoned it was round about the mark. . . .'

'It's perfect, Dutt. It's the one I'd have chosen myself.'

'The Missus thought as how you might like a change, but I never see you smoke nothing different. . . .'

'I wouldn't, Dutt, not if anyone paid me. And while we're on the subject of presents, there are some things here for the Missus, you and the kids.'

He pulled open the door of one of the cupboards under the bookcase and revealed a giant Christmas stocking. It was packed very tight, and looked excitingly nobbly, and the label that floated from it was cut in the shape of a dangling pair of handcuffs.

'Don't open it now . . . it'd take too long. By the way, what size was it you said the Missus took?'

Dutt clasped the stocking to him grotesquely, something suspiciously like moisture in his eye. 'Thanks, sir . . . you're one of the best! The kiddies are going to miss you coming round, sir.'

'I'm going to miss them too . . . but I'll look in when I get back. You'll be having a party at New Year, won't you?'

'Yessir—I got a split duty.'

'All right then, that's a date.'

They stood for some moments in silence, one each side of the lazy flames. Down below the paper-boy was going his rounds, and footfalls sounded sharply on the frosty pavement. Gently pulled two cigars from his breast-pocket and shoved one of them into Dutt's mouth.

'Come on. . . . I've got to go. It's me for the wide-open spaces '

Dutt nodded and scratched a light for them. 'You won't have to phone for a taxi, sir.'

'Won't have to . . . why not, Dutt?'

''Cause I got a Jag outside, sir.' The Sergeant grinned at him guiltily. 'It was going spare in the garage, sir, I reckoned nobody wasn't going to miss it for an hour. . . .'

Gently shook his head with mock gravity. 'You'll wind up bashing a beat, Dutt my lad! But since it's here, we'd better not waste the Yard's petrol. Get hold of that suitcase, and let's try to look as though we own a Jag anyway.'

In spite of himself, Gently couldn't help feeling a mild thrill of excitement as he and Dutt, laden with luggage and the precious pike-rod, plunged into the icy pandemonium of Liverpool Street Station. So many people going home—going home for Christmas! There were queues at every platform and every ticket-window, surging crowds of people, burdened, like himself, with suit-cases, parcels, Christmas-trees, everything under the sun. How could one fail to catch the spirit? How could one be chilled by the cold, or depressed by the great, dark, sooty vaults of the station which echoed above the seething crowds below? Home for Christmas! All of London seemed to be in one mind. Pack your things—catch a train. Leave the streets and shop-windows, soon to be shuttered, leave the gloomy world of offices and work and worry. All that was over. A truce had been called. Now one could lock the door and forget the shabbiness, one could hasten to meet old friends, to renew oneself in the heart of the family. Catch a train, come home for Christmas!

Gently wasn't going home, but he was too sensitive to atmospheres long to resist this one. Well . . . perhaps it wasn't going to be so bad, after all! There were other sorts of Christmases besides the one he had made a habit of. And it might do him good to have a change, to see how it was with other people. . . .

The queue for the 'Northshireman' was already moving through the barrier. In his pocket he had an unaccustomed luxury, a first-class ticket.

'Anything to read on the train, sir?' Dutt motioned to the book-stall.

'Everything they've got, Dutt! I don't often go away for Christmas.'

An armful of expensive Christmas supplements was added to his load.

'All right for tobacco, sir?'

'One of those half-pound tins . . . and wait a minute! Some cigars. One can't go empty-handed.'

All the way down the platform he added to his store. A sudden urge to lavishness overcame his customary frugality. Wasn't this the time to spend, with the turkey round the corner?

'Get me some fruit, Dutt—oh, and one of those boxes of chocolate . . . how about crystallized ginger? Get two, and take one home.'

He wouldn't starve, at all events. As far as he was concerned, that train could now stick fast in a snowdrift. Struggling with the evidence of his extravagance, he got out the first-class ticket and waved it at the man on the barrier. Christmas with the upper crust—one had to make a gesture here and there.

The seat he had booked was in a compartment close to the barrier, and he was rather sorry to see that, in spite of the queue, he looked like having it to himself. In his present mood he wanted company. He wanted to keep himself immersed in the hurrying, scurrying current of home-bound people. But the train was filling up, and still he was the lone occupant. It looked as though first-class travel was getting to be a thing of the past.

' 'Fraid I'll have to go, sir.'

'You'd better, Dutt, and get that confounded Jag back in its garage.'

'Well . . . have a good time, sir. And a Merry Christmas from one and all.'

'Same to you Dutt, and many of them.'

He watched the burly form of the Sergeant disappear through the crowd, and then sat down away from the window to make it quite clear that the compartment had vacant seats. Damn it all . . . there couldn't be such a dearth of first-class custom going this way! Surely a late-comer would materialize from somewhere . . . ?

'Say . . . is that train going to Norchester?'

He heard the American accents coming all the way from the barrier.

'Hurry? You bet I'll hurry! What have I been doing all the way from Oxford Street?'

Gently jumped up and whisked open the door.

'Here!' he called out, 'there's a seat here.'

A lanky figure, stooping low under its parcels, came bolting up the now-empty platform. Gently stood aside to give it passage. At the same moment the whistle shrilled and the 'Northshireman' began to glide out.

'Hell!' ejaculated the sprawling American, 'who says these goddam Britishers don't know how to get a hustle-on?'

Straightfaced, Gently gave him a hand up and helped him to organize his scattered parcels. He was a young man of about twenty-three, and although he couldn't much have over-topped Gently's six feet, he seemed big enough to fill up most of the compartment.

'Hell!' he exclaimed again, 'hell!' Then he grinned at Gently suddenly. 'Don't you pay any attention to me, sir. Guess I'm just three parts riled with myself, that's about it.'

'You ran short of time?' suggested Gently affably.

'You can say that again—and again and again!'

'It's a bit of a rush up here at Christmas.'

'A bit of a rush . . . ! Sir, you can put that down as the British Understatement of the Year.'

He brushed himself off, and, unconscious of Gently's amused scrutiny, settled his fluffy brown hair with a comb. He had a pleasant, button-nosed face with a square jaw and chin, his eyes were hazel, and he had very white, even teeth.

'Do you know something?' he demanded, catching Gently's eye over the mirror he was using.

Gently looked suitably inquisitive.

'Well, this is the first time I've been in this city of yours—yes sir, the very first time. And man, did I underestimate it or did I?'

Gently clicked his tongue sympathetically. 'It'll be quieter in a day or two.'

'Lit in here, I did, like a hick from the backwoods. Sure, I was going to do my Christmas shopping. Sure, I was going to have it all sewn up in half a day. And do you know something else?'

Gently shook his head.

'I didn't do that Christmas shopping—I didn't do the best half of it! One moment I was being shoved around that Selfridge's like a steer in a stampede, next thing I know my train was due out in fifteen minutes. I ask you, where does time go to in this place? How do people ever get around to what they aim to do? I guess there's only one thing left for this city, sir—you'll have to done go and build some scrapers to get the folk up off the streets!'

Gently considered this solution seriously for a moment. 'That's a new idea for the planners, at all events,' he replied.

'You bet,' said the American, intent on his parting, 'it's no good shoving the people out sideways.'

The north-east suburbs were crawling by on either hand, frosty deserts of streets and yards, dusted and parcelled with misty light. Hatched along the line came row after row of wretched slum-properties, their obscene backs lit dimly from uncurtained windows. Fascinated, Gently watched the shameful pageant unfold. The imagination faltered at the sheer extent of such misery. Not a few hundred yards, not a mile, not two; it went on and on, district melting into district. Who would value honesty, trapped in that jungle?

'Me, I'm Lieutenant William S. Earle of the United States Air Force.'

The American had got his packages on the seat and was sorting through them anxiously.

'Me, I'm George H. Gently, Chief Inspector, C.I.D., Central Office,' returned Gently with a smile.

'A Chief Inspector, huh?' Earle said it as though Chief Inspectors meant nothing in his young life. 'Well, I guess it takes all sorts. You going home for Christmas?'

'No . . . not exactly. Someone invited me to stay.'

'That's nice, very nice. Me, I've got an invitation too. I'm having me a Christmas with a real live British Lord—can you beat it? Right there on his estate out in the country, and man, when I say estate I *mean* estate! He's got a place back there would make an oil king throw fits.'

Gently made polite noises.

'Yes sir! Fits it would make him throw, and no two ways. But maybe you've heard of this guy. They call him Lord Somerhayes. Naturally, he's got other names too, but once you get to be a Lord, well then I guess you just drop all the smaller stuff and leave it at that. You heard his name before?'

'Yes, I think so.'

'I reckoned you would have, too. And maybe you've heard of his estate, huh?'

'Isn't that in Northshire somewhere?'

'You're darned right it is, plumb in the middle. And you know something else? We've got an airfield called Sculton not ten miles off, and that's how Lieutenant William Sherwood Earle comes to be having himself a Christmas with a British Lord.'

Having, as it were, established his bona fides, Earle offered Gently a cigar, and then took time off to brood over the seat-full of packages beside him. They were getting out of the slum area now. Dark gaps were appearing in the laval deposit of slate, bricks and dirt. With surprising frequency long, well-lighted platforms swung out of the darkness and flashed by before one could catch the name-boards . . . the 'Northshireman' was picking up her easy, space-destroying stride. Gently settled himself back more comfortably on the generous first-class cushions. Why should he spoil the rare pleasure by tormenting himself with the imagined wretchedness of the dwellers in that petrified forest? It might be better than one envisaged . . . there were occasional television aerials. If people could afford television, surely they could afford to leave a district uncongenial to them? He thought of Dutt's noisy terrace house at Tottenham. The back of that row would probably look like slum property, and certainly there wasn't a shred of privacy. But Dutt didn't care, nor did his neighbors, and nor, Gently recollected with some surprise, did he either, when he was there amongst it. It was all an attitude of mind. If you were brought up as a member of a semi-communal society, you would probably feel lonely and naked in a detached house in a fenced garden.

'Say, are you married, Gently?'

Gently came out of his revery to find Earle holding up a frilly, black silk specimen of female underwear.

'No,' he said, 'no. Guess I never was, Earle.'

'Gee, that's a pity. I thought maybe you could help me out over the size of these things.' He inspected the exhibit with naïve admiration. 'Cute, ain't they? I paid nine pounds seven shillings and fourpence halfpenny for these, and I guess that's plenty. You think they will fit a sorta average kind of female?'

Gently gave the matter his attention. 'It's out of my province, but I imagine they probably would.'

'Yeah, that's what the sales-girl reckoned. It's darned difficult when you don't know the lady well enough to ask her measurements. I been going through these things most of the afternoon—guess that must have been where it went to, at that.'

He wrapped the lingerie up carefully in its tissue, and put it away in a flowery carton bearing the name of a famous West End firm.

'But don't get me wrong when I call that female

average, Gently. No sir! There ain't nothing average
about the second cousin of a real live Lord. You mix
with the aristocracy, huh?'

'Not habitually, Earle. I just run across them now
and then.'

'Guess you've seen some of those classy dames,
duchesses and such-like?'

'An occasional duchess, perhaps.'

'Well, a Lord's second cousin don't rate as high as a
duchess, of course, but the quality is there all right,
don't you forget it. I guess once you're in on the
blood, you're in, and it don't signify how many re-
moves you come out at. Wouldn't you say that was a
fact?'

'Guess you would, Earle, at that.'

'And man, this one surely is a peach—and nobody's
kidding nobody. Janice Elizabeth Augusta they call
her, Feverell that was, Page that is. Married to a surgeon, she used to be, but he cashed his chips a couple
of years back.'

'And she's living with her cousin now?'

'She is too. Which is how Lieutenant Earle came to
make her acquaintance. I guess you never did try
your hand at tapestry-weaving, Gently?'

'Tapestry-weaving?' Gently stared at this abrupt
and apparently irrelevant switch of subject.

'Yeah, that's what I said. Tapestry-weaving. Me, I
didn't know it was still going on till maybe a couple
of months back. My old man runs a newspaper back
in Carpetville, Missouri, and either I go on the paper
when I come out or else I don't. Well if I don't I aim
to be a painter—they reckon I've got talent in New
York, where I studied some—but now I've seen this

tapestry-weaving slant I ain't so sure as I was. You follow me okay?'

Gently blinked a little. 'Could be,' he conceded, 'but what's tapestry-weaving got to do with Lord Somerhayes' second cousin?'

'I'm coming to it. I just wanted to put you square with the set-up. Now a couple of months back there's one of those culturals going on in camp, and this guy Brass comes along to chew the rag about tapestry. Well, that was all news to Lieutenant Earle, who used to figure tapestry packed up about the time bows-and-arrows went out. But no sir, not a bit of it. Seems like they'd been turning it out steadily all the time. And this guy Brass, who'd spent a year or two in Paris, had got a workshop good and busy right there in Lord Somerhayes' house. Well, Lieutenant Earle got mightily curious about this business. He got himself invited in to see how the stuff was cooked up. And now he's taking lessons just as often as he can get there, and wondering whether the U.S.A. couldn't use a tapestry workshop.'

'And Lord Somerhayes' second cousin?'

Earle waved his big hands.

'They're all knee-deep in the racket. I guess she helps with the business side. This Brass guy reckons Lord Somerhayes went off the deep end about something that happened in the House of Lords, can you imagine it? So he takes up this tapestry notion by way of giving the House of Lords the air. Sure thing he never sets foot in there these days, though I guess they get along pretty fine without him.'

Earle brooded a moment, frowning at the two inches of ash on the end of his cigar.

'He's a queer sort of buster, the Lord. I just can't get around to figuring him out. But Lord Chesterfield didn't have nothing on him when it comes to class, and time you're a Lord I guess you've a right to act strange. Wouldn't you say that was a fact?'

Gently grinned at the American's puzzled countenance. 'I think you would, Earle,' he said, 'I think you'd definitely say it was a fact.'

Onward thundered the 'Northshireman' through the frost-sharp night. London was far behind them, only now and then did a cluster of lights shine out from the jet-like blackness, or a station briefly startle them with its astral flight. In the swaying compartment it was warm and drowsy. Several times Gently nodded off, to be brought back to consciousness by the sudden rasp of a bridge under which they had flashed, or the roll of the coach as it tore round a curve sharper than usual. Finally he must have dropped right off. He was wakened by a hand shaking his shoulder, and opened his eyes to see Earle standing by him, parcels piled high in the American's arms.

'End of the track, Gently . . . guess you won't get any further on this waggon.'

'Norchester, is it?'

'That's what it says on the boards.'

Gently stretched himself, rose, and began pulling down his cases. Earle was having trouble opening the door with such an armful.

'Well, it's been nice knowing, you, Gently . . . reckon we'll have to skip the handshake. You wouldn't know where I pick up a train for a whistle-stop called Merely?'

Gently smiled into the distant reaches of the night.

'It's this one on the opposite platform. Get a move on or we'll lose it.'

'Hey!' exclaimed Earle, 'you wouldn't be coming that way too?'

'I would, Lieutenant. All the way to Merely.'

'But jeez, there's nothing there except the station-hut and the Lord's!'

'There's also the Manor House, Lieutenant . . . you must have overlooked it. I've got the impression that you and I are going to extend our acquaintance.'

CHAPTER TWO

'YOUR MORNING tea, sir?'

Gently prolonged the voluptuous moment of wakening in a superbly warm and comfortable bed. Off duty, that was the happy thought that came to him. No need to leap suddenly from the nurturing bowers of sleep, to race through his toilet, to plunge into the chaotic morning Underground. He was off duty, and miles away. Out here, waking-up was a pleasure worth tasting and lingering over. . . .

'You didn't answer, sir, so I took the liberty of bringing it in.'

He opened an eye. A neat little maid in uniform stood by the bed smiling at him. She was carrying, not a cup, but an interesting-looking bed-tray on which he could see, *inter alia,* copies of *The Times* and the *Eastern Daily Post.* He dragged himself up the bed a few points to receive this consignment. The atmosphere of the room was pleasantly warm, and he remembered with appreciation that the amenities of Merely Manor included central heating.

'How's the weather outside . . . ?'

'Oh, there's a nip in the air, sir, but it's quite dry.'

'Pike weather, would you say?'

'I don't rightly know, sir, but the Master and some of his friends have got some big 'uns this last week or two. Will you want your bath run, sir?'

'Mmm . . . all hot. By the time I'm through here it'll be about right.'

The maid dropped a polite little curtsey and tripped away into the bathroom, from which direction Gently could soon hear the steady swish of water, and see the occasional tendril of steam. He unbonneted the pot and poured himself a fragrant cupful. Under a plated cover he found some fingers of toast, on a plate were some wholemeal biscuits. He chose the former, and dismissing yesterday's resolution, settled down to peruse his papers.

Christmas . . . that was the subject! On the back page of *The Times* was a large photograph of King's Cross looking like an illimitable bargain-basement at a peak period. The local paper, not to be outdone, had contrived a panoramic shot of Norchester Thorne Station in a similar state of chaos. QUEUES AT ALL THE LONDON TERMINI—Biggest Exodus Ever. LARGEST TEMPORARY POST-OFFICE STAFF. STILL SOME TURKEYS LEFT—Consignment from Eire. 100-FOOT XMAS TREE. BRITISH RAILWAYS RUN 200 EXTRA TRAINS. TROOPSHIP ARRIVES FROM MIDDLE EAST. . . . Gently surveyed it all with a benevolent smile. Up here, it was like a well-calculated performance laid on for his especial benefit. No longer was he a part of it. No longer was it an anxious time of probable trial and tribulation. Sipping his tea, he could savour the whole business as an idle spectator, with undercurrent thoughts of a day to be spent pike-fishing. . . .

'It's all ready for you, sir.'

'Thank you . . . what's your name?'

'Gertrude, sir. Gertrude Winfarthing.'

'That's a nice name, Gertrude. Well . . . thanks again!'

She bobbed out, still smiling, and Gently, setting the tray on a bedside table, lowered his feet on to the gratifying pile of a Wilton carpet. He paused there a moment, letting his eye run round the gracious room. By and large, this was how things ought to be. A wide, lofty, well-lighted chamber, with a moulded drop-ceiling, panelled walls, a great sunken sash-window and white enamelled woodwork. The carpet went flush to the walls, the velvet curtains hung from ceiling to floor. The bed, disdaining the beggarly excuse of functionalism, spread extravagant panels of natural oak at head and foot, and the matching wardrobe standing near it seemed quietly to rejoice in its spreading amplitude. What was wrong with idle riches? There were times when one deserved them. Man, as the ancient writer had shrewdly noticed, could not live by bread alone. . . .

Disdaining his slippers, Gently plodded across to the bathroom and was soon up to his chin in delicately-scented water.

He had seen Sir Daynes the night before, but Lady Broke had already retired, and he met her now at breakfast for the first time. She was a tallish, large-framed woman of something over fifty, with greying hair, quick, green-brown eyes and a Roman nose which gave her a quite unmerited appearance of severity. One expected to hear her bark in the manner of her formidable husband, but she did not, she

had a soft, confiding voice; one saw very quickly that
a great deal of sensitivity lay behind the austere countenance.

'Good morning, Inspector . . . I hope you've for-
given me for not being up to welcome you last night.'

She smiled at him as she gave him her hand.

'I'd been very busy, you know—you'd be surprised
at the preparation that goes on here! Even now the
children have grown up and left us, there seems as
much to do as ever. Were you properly looked after?'

Gently liked her straight away. They were soon
chatting together like old friends. Before Sir Daynes
put in an appearance she had shown him letters from
her son Tony, a young officer in the Malaya Police,
and her daughter Elizabeth, who had married a Cana-
dian and was now living in Toronto.

'There'll be cables from them too, either to-day or
to-morrow. It's so strange, Inspector, to think that
both my youngsters should be at the ends of the earth,
while I go on here just the same, getting ready for another Christmas. This is the first time we've been
quite on our own, you know, I was so glad when Sir
Daynes thought of asking you down.'

'I am honoured to be invited, ma'am.'

'Oh, that was inevitable. My husband has got a
"thing" about you, Inspector. But be frank—weren't
you a little annoyed by his high-handed way of getting you down here, right on top of Christmas? Personally I should have been furious if he'd done
something like that to me.'

Gently grinned amiably. 'Of course, knowing Sir
Daynes——'

'Enough said, Inspector. My husband has been a

Chief Constable for too long, isn't that what you'd say? But do sit down and begin your breakfast. It's quite useless waiting for Daynes.'

Sir Daynes joined them at the marmalade stage, looking very crisp and new-minted. To Gently, he had always been the type *par excellence* of a county Chief Constable. Going six feet, he was still, at sixty, a strong, commanding figure without one of his grey hairs missing. His face was powerful, a large, straight nose, heavy grey brows, cropped moustache and distinguished lines about the eyes and mouth. There was a great deal of width across the cheek-bones and jaw. The large head looked patriarchal and ripe with sapience. Though case-hardened Supers had been known to wince when Sir Daynes was in full cry, Gently had several times had occasion to notice the absence of bite behind the baronet's bark.

'Morning Gwen, morning Gently.'

Sir Daynes was carrying a deckle-edged sheet of writing paper, over which he was frowning absent-mindedly.

'Hmn.' He sat down, still staring at it. 'Henry Somerhayes. Wants us to go over there.'

'Henry?' queried Lady Broke, pouring coffee into his cup.

'Hmn. Informal party. To-night at seven-thirty. Why couldn't the blasted feller have thought about it earlier?'

He dropped sugar into his coffee and shot a sharp look at Gently. '*You* wouldn't be the reason, I suppose? He's made a special point of mentioning you.'

Gently began to shake his head, but then he remembered Lieutenant Earle.

'I travelled down with a guest of Lord Somerhayes
... my name may have been mentioned to him.'

'Ah, that explains it. You're a blasted lion in these
parts, man. Well, what do you say to a Christmas Eve
with his Lordship?'

Gently acquiesced, and Sir Daynes drank his coffee.
From his attitude it seemed that he did not approve
too highly of his neighbour.

'Henry Somerhayes is a curious person,' ventured
Lady Broke, 'we think it is a great pity he didn't
marry, Inspector. He's very much alone in the world.'

'Curious!' snorted Sir Daynes. 'Damned unhealthy,
I'd call him. But there you are, a man's got a right to
do what he thinks fit with himself.'

'Oh come now,' returned his wife, 'you'll give the
Inspector a totally wrong impression of him. I'm sure
that if Henry could find himself the right woman
he'd be quite a different sort of person. When you've
lost all your family, as he has, it makes you broody
and apt to take things to heart. And really you've
nothing against him, Daynes, except his retreat from
politics.'

'It's enough,' said Sir Daynes, 'that and the crowd
he's got up at the Place these days. But I won't say
any more. Gently can take him as he finds him. Let's
talk about the fishing, and forget Henry until this
evening.'

They talked about the fishing. Sir Daynes was a
live-bait practitioner, and Gently a spoon-man, and
between them they managed to consign Lord Somerhayes to oblivion inside five minutes. An hour later,
booted and armed, they set off through the December
gloom for Merely Pond, where Gently had the good

fortune to prove the efficacy of the spoon up to the hilt.

'Damned detectives ought to make good fishermen!' observed Sir Daynes enviously as Gently gaffed his sixth fish. 'But I tell you, man, you've struck a lucky day. Blasted pike aren't looking at live-bait, for some reason. Another day they wouldn't look at a damned spoon. . . .'

Gently smiled agreeably as he inserted the disgorger.

The frost was setting in sharp as they returned to the Manor. Red brick Georgian, it glowed warmly in its setting of tall beeches, smoke rising straight from its twisted stacks, lights shining comfortably in the high windows.

'Wish we hadn't got to shift. . . .'

Gently was thinking so too. Glutted with their sport, and tired, it would have been pleasant to spend the evening chatting by the wood fire in the Manor lounge.

'Damn that feller Somerhayes! Ought to have told him we couldn't make it.'

'After all, it's Christmas. . . .'

'Some people take advantage of it.'

But after a whisky Sir Daynes felt better about the business. He began remembering Christmases when the old Lord had been alive. From that it was a short step to bragging about the Place, the finest thing Kent ever did, and to wanting Gently to see it and judge with his own eyes. By the time they had had tea, and Lady Broke had exerted her soothing influence, Sir Daynes was in a mood of charity suitable to a Christmas Eve party.

*   *   *

Gently could never remember exactly what had
been his first impression of Lord Somerhayes. The
meeting took place in the Great Hall of Merely Place,
and the Great Hall, for those who had never seen it,
was apt to set aside mere humanity while it consoli-
dated its regal impact. It was all the more stunning
for being unexpected. Driving up in Sir Daynes'
Bentley, Gently had made out little of the outside architecture of Merely except its size, which the lighted
windows had intimated. The headlights had picked
out a plain, rather flat-looking Doric portico as the
Bentley swung round on the terrace, and through a
single door beneath this they had been admitted by a
manservant. It was then that a sparely-built man of
about forty had come forward and welcomed them
with a little, self-conscious smile; but against the sudden soaring divinities of the Great Hall he had faded
into a spectral undertone.

It was a vast, magical rectangle of space, perhaps as
high as it was long, and more than half its length in
width. Far overhead rose a great coffered ceiling, be-
wildering in its perspective, narrowing at the far end
to a clasping, semi-circular apse; supporting this was
a range of fluted Corinthian columns, linked at their
base by richly-gilt wrought-iron pales, and beneath
them a glowing foundation of polished marble decorated with Hellenic friezes, embracing beneath the
apse a fall of curved steps which seemed to flow down
from the marble portal above. The detail was no less
rich than the broad features. The plaster-work of the
ceiling, the triumphant frieze above the columns, the
illuminated azure and gilt secondary apse above the
portal, all these contributed like so many matching

trumpet voluntaries to the overpowering vision of the whole. Here, surely, was one of those rare examples when the genius of a great artist found its full and unqualified expression, the fortunate one occasion of an ambitious life.

At all events, it bowled Gently over. His impressions of what followed were vague. They were led through a tremendous suite of rooms, icy as the tomb, and came at last to a less-magnificent but decidedly warmer chamber where a yule-log burned on the hearth, and a handful of people paused in their conversation to observe the newcomers.

'What will you drink, Mr. Gently?'

Gently was startled to find a pair of sad, grey-blue eyes staring fixedly into his.

'Oh—a whisky, please.'

'Good. You will like this whisky. I have it sent down each year from Edinburgh. May I recommend a petticoat-tail to go with it?'

'Yes . . . yes please.'

'They are also sent down from Edinburgh. They are baked by Mackie to a special recipe.'

Equipped with liqueur and short-bread, Gently was marshalled with Sir Daynes and Lady Broke to meet the other guests. Already he had an inexplicable feeling that Lord Somerhayes was distinguishing him in some way. It was not so much a matter of attention, for Somerhayes distributed it evenly; but in the manner of it there was a distinct singularity which Gently was at a loss to place.

'Janice, you already know Sir Daynes and Lady Broke. This is Mr. Gently, the Chief Inspector from the Central Office. Mr. Gently, my cousin Mrs. Page, who is kind enough to act as my secretary.'

As Gently shook hands with the queenly ash-blonde he felt Somerhayes' eyes covertly watching him.

'Lieutenant Earle's acquaintance you have already made. . . .'

'Hiya, you old hound!' interpolated the irrepressible American.

'. . . and this is Leslie Brass, the director, I may say creator, of the tapestry workshop. But no doubt you will have heard of Mr. Brass and perhaps have seen his pictures.'

This time Gently was painfully aware of his host's silent scrutiny, and at the same time he caught a glimpse of irony in the bold green eyes of the artist to whom he was being introduced. Brass had noticed Somerhayes' curious attitude. More than that, Gently thought he had understood it.

'And these very talented people are the *tapissiers* who actually produce the tapestry. Miss Hepstall and Miss Jacobs are ex-pupils of Mr. Brass. Mr. Johnson joined us from Wales. Mr. and Mrs. Peacock are Lancashire people, and Mr. Wheeler comes from Yorkshire.'

But now the keenness had left Somerhayes' glance, he did not seem so interested in what Gently would make of the *tapissiers*. Perhaps, in spite of his graciousness, the nobleman did not regard them as important—his short list terminated with Mrs. Page, Leslie Brass, and possibly Lieutenant Earle. At all events, he was obliged to relinquish Gently for the moment. Lady Broke claimed him with the acknowledged freedom of a neighbour, and Gently, set at liberty, was immediately seized by Lieutenant Earle.

'Say now, come and meet these nice people properly —neither one of them has run across a man from Scotland Yard before!'

Gently smiled and joined the group over by the fire. Earle was sitting on a long settee with Mrs. Page; Brass, an enormous man with ginger hair and beard, was sunk deeply in an armchair beside them. Gently pulled up a straight-backed chair.

'Now, was I wrong when I said Janice was the next contender for the Miss Universe title, or was I guilty of understatement?'

Mrs. Page blushed slightly but didn't look displeased. She was a woman in her later twenties and she had the same eyes as her cousin—except that in her case they possessed a vitality and sparkle. The nose was straight and finely nostrilled, the cheek-bones high, the complexion exquisitely transparent. She had very beautiful lips and a long white neck, a feature which she emphasized by wearing drooping jade ear-drops from pierced ears. Her figure was moderate but proportioned with exact symmetry, and her voice, pitched high, sounded lively and excitable.

'Please pay no attention to this *enfant terrible*, Mr. Gently—we're trying to keep him in order, but I doubt whether the President of the United States himself could manage it.'

'Now Janice, is that fair——!'

'You've really got to *behave*, Bill.'

'Gee, and it's Christmas Eve—don't fellers ever get the pitching in this doggone British festival?'

Brass winked at Gently from the depths of his arm-chair.

'These ruddy young Yankee Casanovas . . . !' He had a vigorous, vibrant voice with a trace of Cockney in it. 'Sex, sex, nothing but sex. You'll say it's all the revolting sex-treacle their radio pumps into them, but is it? Is it? Would the radio, films and other pimps bother about it if they weren't sure of a psychopathic demand?'

'Say, Les, you're talking about the Great American Nation!'

'I certainly am, little Don Juan Doughboy.' Brass ruffled Earle's boyish locks with a sort of contemptu-ous affection. 'God's gift to corruption with a loud voice—America! The Brave New World with a petti-coat rampant! I say your youth is psychopathic, little man, it's got sex on the brain. And you are a fine ex-ample, little Check-with-Kinsey, you prove my point every other time you open your mouth.'

'Now Les, how can you say these things to me!'

'Why not, *petit* sex-fiend?'

'Right here, in front of the people!'

'They are rational, *mon ami,* not one of them comes from Boston.'

'Heck, I give you up!' Earle turned to Gently with a despairing wave of his hand. 'This guy just hates the American Nation, lock, stock, and spittoon—can you imagine it? I tell him if it wasn't for America there wouldn't be nothing interesting going on, like the numbers racket and Billy Graham. But no, he's dug his toes in. That guy has got no gratitood. Guess it'll have to wait till I get him down to Missouri and feed him Southern Style fried chicken.'

'Is that a recipe for America-haters?' enquired Gently with interest.

'Why yes, I'll say it is. The way my momma cooks fried chicken would make an American Citizen out of a top-brass Red. You never been to America, Gently?'

Gently shook his head. 'It's always been on my agenda . . .'

'Sakes, you don't know what you're missing! You come down to Missouri—any time, any day. This old buzzard here is going to make the trip next fall, and Janice hasn't said no to it, leastways not in my hearing.'

Mrs. Page shrugged her shapely shoulders. 'Bill, you talk too much,' she said. 'And if you go on inviting people down to Missouri, you'll have to charter the *Queen Mary* to get them all there. Now be a dear and fetch me another sherry—and I'm sure Mr. Gently would like to have his glass topped up.'

'To hear is to obey, Princess!'

Earle jumped from the settee and knelt gallantly to take Mrs. Page's glass from her.

'The Carpetville Heart-throb!' grinned Brass to Gently, 'but the boy has talent, make no mistake. He's done a cracking good cartoon since he was here last, real tapestry stuff. I'm going to let him use a spare low-warp loom we've got here to weave it on. He's not much of a *tapissier* yet, but spoiling his nice cartoon will teach him plenty. On the quiet I'm going to have a go at it myself . . . it's too good a cartoon to let him waste.'

'I'm afraid this is rather over my head, Mr. Brass,' Gently admitted.

'It won't be,' laughed Mrs. Page, 'not if Les gets his

claws in you. We live and eat and sleep tapestry here, Mr. Gently.'

'So you do, madam, so you do,' assented Brass sardonically. 'It's the only way to produce tapestry. Come up after Christmas, Gently, and I'll show you over the workshop. You have to get the stink of wool in your nostrils before you can understand tapestry.'

Gently agreed readily enough. He felt he would like to have a private session with Brass. All the time they had been talking together Somerhayes' glances had kept wandering in their direction, and Gently was reasonably certain that Brass could offer him enlightenment. What *was* the enigmatic nobleman's interest in him? Surely he wasn't being carried away by the glamour of Gently's 'Yard' tag! Under the cover of filling Dutt's pipe, Gently unobtrusively quizzed his host, adding detail to his rather confused impression of him. Assuredly there was the stamp of high breeding in his features. The high, straight forehead, the perfectly chiselled nose, the high cheekbones instinct with pride, the thin-lipped mouth, the small, graceful chin and jaw, the neat, close-set ears, all these combined to give an immediate effect of nobility. It was the eyes that spoiled the picture. They lacked the fire which should have brought the whole to life. Large, handsome, evenly set beneath strongly-marked brows, their dominant characteristic was a pensive languor, as though the man behind them were tired and brought to a standstill by disillusions. They were the eyes of one who had already accepted his defeat from life.

'Sir Daynes beef much about coming this evening?'

The cynical look told Gently that Brass had observed the direction of his attention.

'He doesn't like me, you know. I'm blasted peasantry. If you think the world has moved on much in these parts, you're ruddy well mistaken. Up here it's the last stronghold of mediævalism.'

'Les, I won't have that!' exclaimed Mrs. Page with warmth. 'When did you ever experience any snobbery, here at the Place?'

'Oh, I don't say at the Place, my dear'—Brass's cynical look renewed itself—'the Place is a beacon-light of social enlightenment in a wicked County world . . . or something like that! But dear old Sir Daynes gets restive when he has to hob-nob with the hoi polloi. We're all right in Bethnal Green, but gad sir! Not in the drawing-room at Merely.'

'I think you're wrong, Les,' returned Mrs. Page. 'You often mistake people. I've known Sir Daynes longer than you, and I assure you I've never found him the least bit of a snob.'

'I'm sure you haven't, Janice my pet. Why should you, with the blood of the Feverells running in your veins? But if you watch Sir Daynes, you'll see him wince every time Percy Peacock says "thanking-gyou".'

Mrs. Page laughed outright. 'Well, so do I, for that matter—and so do you, when you're being honest. But I suppose you're not going to call me a snob, Les, because I speak English? Bill doesn't, and he's a Great American Democrat.'

'You taking my name in vain?' sang the latter, coming up and presenting Mrs. Page's glass with a flourish which nearly spilled the contents. 'Don't deny it—I heard you! My reputation is mud with the Britishers.'

At the sound of Earle's voice, Gently noticed Somerhayes' head turn sharply.

Supper was served in the adjoining dining-room. It was a well-chosen but moderate meal, restrained as though it were intended to look forward to the excesses of the morrow. Gently found himself placed next to his host, but the circumstances led to nothing. Somerhayes attended to him with a sort of earnest graciousness. He seemed always on the point of saying something, without being able to bring it out. And whenever Gently raised his eyes, he was sure to meet those of the other, watchful, apologetic.

After supper some games were organized. Brass was particularly good at that sort of thing, and he was soon installed as master of ceremonies. For assistant he had Percy Peacock, the comical little bald-headed Lancastrian, while Earle could be relied upon to give zest to any festive undertaking. Even Sir Daynes and Lady Broke were drawn into the fun. Sir Daynes, set to mime a lachrymose crooner, displayed histrionic powers which surprised everyone, including himself. Brass was rather disappointed, Gently thought . . . the artist had deliberately given Sir Daynes a forfeit which was calculated to make a fool of him. But Brass was soon in the midst of fresh revelry, Sir Daynes with him, and the proceedings went forward like the wedding-bell of proverb. Only one person held back. Somerhayes, a glass of port in his hand, stood silently watching by the hearth with its half-consumed log. He had relinquished his command. He had handed over to Brass. Until goodbyes were to be said, there was no more occasion for the master of Merely Place.

Soon after half-past eleven Lady Broke reminded her husband that this was Christmas Eve, not Christmas Night, and the roistering baronet was prevailed upon to adjourn his revels.

'Say, pop, we've sure got to see some more of you!' cried Earle enthusiastically. 'What say we get together again for a session on Boxing Day?'

'Young man, I've a better idea,' returned Sir Daynes, clapping him on the shoulder. 'Henry, I shall be most offended if you fail to bring your people over to the Manor the day after to-morrow. That's a Chief Constable's order, man, and as much as your life is worth to dispute. What do you say—will you come?'

Somerhayes came forward, his thin lips twisting in a slow smile. 'If it's an order, Daynes, how can I do myself the disservice of refusing?'

'Yippee!' whooped Earle, 'it's a date, you old horse-thief! We'll surely set that Manor of yours alight, and nobody's kidding.'

Somerhayes turned to Gently. 'And I shall have the pleasure of another visit from you, Mr. Gently, before long? I should be very happy to show you over the state apartments and our workshop.'

Gently mastered his surprise. There was something very like an appeal in the broken grey eyes.

'Certainly . . . I'll be pleased to come,' he replied.

Somerhayes nodded his acknowledgement and turned hastily away.

'Well, I must say they're not a bad crowd, not bad at all,' boomed Sir Daynes as he gunned the Bentley down the Place carriage-drive. 'You get ideas in your head, Inspector, and sometimes they take a lot of shifting. That Brass feller is a lad, give the devil his due. And I like that young American, with all his blasted impertinence.'

'Don't leave out the little blonde girl with the pony-tail,' said Lady Broke. 'Isn't it shocking, Inspector, how a man of three score can flirt with a little chit young enough to be his grand-daughter?'

'Pooh, pooh! Christmas Eve, m'dear,' chortled her husband. 'Once a year, y'know, once a year! And I didn't notice you holding back when that young Wheeler feller was going round with the mistletoe, eh? But what do you make of Henry Somerhayes, Gently, now you've had a good look at him?'

Gently shrugged invisibly in his voluptuous bucket-seat.

'I'd have to have notice of that question,' he replied.

CHAPTER THREE

IT WAS IN the middle of breakfast when the telephone call came. Before then, Christmas had proceeded at the Manor with all its customary detail and ceremony.

Quite early in the morning Gently had been awakened by the sound of stirrings about the house and by distant, smothered laughter. Then he had heard the sound of bells ringing in the direction of Upfield-cum-Merely, nearly two miles off, and Gertrude, looking rather red and mischievous, had knocked on the door to ask him if he wanted to go to early morning service.

'Are Sir Daynes and Lady Broke going?'

'Oh yes, sir. Sir Daynes will read the lesson.'

'Righto—run the bath. I'll have my cuppa afterwards.'

The bath was run and Gertrude departed, after exchanging a Merry Christmas with him. By the time he had dressed she was at his door again with tea and a hot mince-pie.

'I beg your pardon, sir. . . .'

'What is it, Gertrude?'

'Well sir, just come and see what's happened outside your door . . . !'

Gently duly went to see, and there surely never was
a more demure Gertrude than the one who pointed
out the little sprig of mistletoe which was pinned to
the transom. Gently sent the baggage about her
business in the approved fashion and appeared below
stairs with a Christmas twinkle in his eye.

Then followed the drive through the dull and
frosted Christmas morning, with the slated sky hanging low over the shallowly undulating fields and still,
sepia groups of trees. The ploughed land looked pale
under the frost, the smoke rose straight from the
chimney of cottage and farm-house. On their way
they met nobody except the labouring postman, red-
faced and steaming in spite of the nipping air, and
for him Sir Daynes pulled up to bestow a Christmas-
box and the compliments of the season.

'Wonder where Henry went this morning,' observed
the baronet as they were returning. 'Usually comes to
Upfield. Felt sure I'd see the feller.'

'He's probably gone to Wrentford,' suggested Lady
Broke. 'It's a good deal nearer to the Place, Daynes.'

'Blasted high church!' returned Sir Daynes irrele-
vantly.

In the breakfast-room a notable fire was blazing,
and a Christmas ham, bread-crumbed and frilled, occupied a place of honour on the well-furnished table.
But first came the presents, in which Gently had not
been forgotten, and then the opening of cards and
letters and the cables from Singapore and Toronto.
Then the plum-porridge was brought in, the same
with which the Man-in-the-Moon had erstwhile burnt

his mouth, and finally Sir Daynes inserted a knife into that monstrous and delicate ham. At which point, with malicious timing, the telephone rang.

'Damn!' said Sir Daynes, and laid down the carvers.

Minutes later he returned, to stand uncertainly in the doorway.

'What is it, Daynes?' enquired Lady Broke anxiously. 'Surely they're not going to call you out to-day?'

Sir Daynes shook his head. He seemed at a loss to find words. Then he came into the room and stood staring curiously at Gently.

'Of all the blasted things to happen!' There was something like a tremor in his customarily aggressive voice. 'That impertinent young American who was going to set the Manor alight . . . well, he's dead. They found his body this morning. Seems as though he took a tumble down the stairway in the Great Hall. . . . I've just been talking to Henry Somer-hayes, and he'd like both of us to come straight over.'

'I'd sooner have kept you out of this.'

Sir Daynes was driving viciously, and the Bentley was his car for the job.

'The press have only got to get a smell of you, Gently, and they'll dream up all sorts of nonsense.'

Gently nodded gloomily. 'In addition to which he's a United States citizen.'

'Exactly, man. There'll be trouble enough without adding fuel to it. In a way it's a damn' good job it's Christmas. They won't be able to print a line until the day after to-morrow. But you can see what they'll make of it—American Serviceman found dead in

Peer's Country Seat. What would be the use of telling them that you were simply a guest of mine?'

Gently nodded again. He felt numbed by the whole business. In a short while he seemed really to have got to know Earle, to have acquired a personal interest in the boisterous young man. And he *had* been so young. Young, ardent, and with all of a fascinating world just opening to him . . . 'either I go on the paper when I come out or else I don't.' How long would it be before a cable silenced the festivities in far-away Missouri?

'D'you think he was drunk last night?'

'No . . . not when we left.'

'He may have got high after that. The post-mortem will tell us something.'

'I don't think he drank a lot. He didn't drink on the train coming up.'

Sir Daynes snorted, as though he felt Gently might have supported such a useful proposition. They whirled through the Place gates and soared zestfully up the serpentine carriage-way. The great yellow-brick front of the Place began to reveal itself through the groves of holm-oak which Repton had planted there with such apparent casualness.

'Just one thing, Gently.' Sir Daynes flashed him a warning look. 'We'd better get it straight—there's been no suggestion of foul play. Personally I can't think of anyone at the Place who'd want to do this young fellow an injury, and I don't want you poking around as though someone had. You don't mind me being frank?'

Gently shook his head.

'Good,' said Sir Daynes with satisfaction. 'This is

going to be a delicate business, and I want to handle it in my own way.'

Two cars stood parked on the terrace as the Bentley came sweeping up, both of them Wolseleys of the type favoured by the local constabulary. Under the restrained portico stood a constable, slowly rocking on his heels, looking like an icicle in spite of his buttoned-up top-coat. He marched stiffly down the steps and opened the door for Sir Daynes.

'Woolston is it?'

'Yes sir, that's me.'

'What the devil is the meaning of this cavalcade, Woolston?'

The constable looked bewildered. 'It's Inspector Dyson, sir. He's got the surgeon and Sergeant Turner with him.'

'What the blasted hell for? Someone pinched the crown jewels? And get inside that door, man, you can guard it quite as well in the hall.'

Up the steps strode Sir Daynes, Gently and the squashed constable in his wake. The Hall, unlit today, looked shadowed and gloomy, but just as they entered there was a hissing flash, and a lurid light reached momentarily to the distant corners. At the foot of the stairs stood a group of six men in an irregular semi-circle, one of them playing with a camera and tripod. In the centre of the semi-circle lay a still, dark, sprawling star-fish, near it a navy blanket which had apparently been used as a cover. Sir Daynes stormed up to this group like a lion pouncing on its prey.

'Dyson!' he barked, 'Dyson! What in the blue blazes is all this tomfoolery?'

A tall, thin-faced man with buck-teeth spun round as though he had been bitten.

'Ah—ah—I beg your pardon, sir?' he stammered.

'This!' fulminated Sir Daynes, with an inclusive sweep of his arm. 'What is it, man? What are you playing at? Why have you got these fellows here?'

Poor Dyson gaped and swallowed and ran a tongue over his divorced upper lip. 'I—I—we were called in, sir. Matter of routine. . . .'

'Routine be beggared! Do you have to turn out a homicide team to take particulars of an accidental death? Why, man, a blasted constable would have done. Wasn't I there, living right next door? Why didn't you get in touch with me?'

'Well sir . . . Christmas Day. . . .'

'Don't talk to me of Christmas Day, Dyson!' Sir Daynes was withering in his wrath. 'As far as the police are concerned there's only one day—a twenty-four hour day—and I happen to be the Chief of Police in these parts. Now get these men out of here. When they're wanted, *I'll* send for them. You stay here—and you, Doctor Shiel. The rest of you get back to your duties or your Christmas pudding—whatever it was you were pulled away from.'

'But sir . . .'

Dyson made a desperate effort to get a word in.

'You heard my orders, Dyson!'

'Sir . . . Doctor Shiel. . . .'

'I have already asked Doctor Shiel to remain.'

'But sir . . . the circumstances . . .'

It looked rather as though Dyson was going to

catch another blast from the Broke thunder-box. Sir Daynes' chin came up and his eyes sparkled pure fire. But just then a slim figure detached itself from the outskirts of the group and intervened between the Inspector and his fate.

'Excuse me, Daynes, but I believe we cannot dispose of this matter quite so simply.'

It was Somerhayes, his handsome face pale, a dry flatness in his cultivated voice.

'Eh, eh?' Sir Daynes turned from the flinching Dyson. 'Henry—didn't see you there, man. Damn it, I'm sorry this place has been turned into a bear-garden for you—blasted mistake, man. I'll soon have them out.'

'There has been no mistake, Daynes.'

'What? Of course there's been a mistake.'

'No, Daynes. The Inspector came at my request. You will appreciate that as a magistrate I had no option but to take what steps seemed necessary.'

Sir Daynes stared at the nobleman as though he had taken leave of his senses. Somerhayes managed to summon up a frosty smile.

'I omitted to tell you on the phone, Daynes, that I had some doubt as to the way in which Earle came by his injuries.'

'Doubt?' echoed Sir Daynes.

'Yes. I could not feel certain in my mind.'

'But you said he'd taken a tumble, and if that's where you found him, by George'—Sir Daynes poked a finger at the spread-eagled body—'then he *did* take a tumble. You aren't going to tell me that somebody pushed him?'

'No . . . I don't think he was pushed.'

'Then what are your doubts about?'

Slowly and without emotion Somerhayes pointed to the skull. The body was lying on its face, the head twisted to one side. Clearly visible at the upper part of the back of the skull was a broad, depressed fracture running in a vertical line. Sir Daynes stared at it grimly, making sure he was missing nothing.

'Well? What's so mysterious about it? Didn't he fall far enough?'

'To fracture his skull—yes. But what caused a fracture like that?'

'Why, man, the answer's obvious. He struck it on a stair. With eighteen or twenty marble stairs to pick from, it's a wonder he had any skull left.'

Somerhayes shook his head. 'There are two things against it, Daynes. The first is the vertical line of the fracture. I cannot think how he could have fallen to have struck his skull backwards and sideways against a stair-edge. The rest of the skull, you will observe, has only abrasions.'

'Balderdash!' snorted Sir Daynes, 'why shouldn't he have struck his head sideways? Anything's possible when a feller comes carreening down one of those things.'

'It may be.' Somerhayes made the ghost of a bow. 'The second point, perhaps, will seem more convincing. It occurred to me when I first saw the body, and Doctor Shiel has come to the same conclusion independently. We find it difficult to understand how this comparatively broad fracture could have been caused by impact with one of these comparatively sharp stair-edges.'

'That is certainly so, Sir Daynes,' put in the police-surgeon, a gaunt-featured Scot, promptly. 'I cannot see at all how the laddie could have done it. If there had been some railings, now, or a good stout ornamental flim-flam of some sort at the foot . . . but as ye see, the stairs just swell out till they reach the sides of the nook. Nothing's here at all to make a dunt like that.'

'That's a matter of opinion!' Sir Daynes' square jaw set in an obstinate line. 'You can't say for certain that a stair-edge wouldn't do it. He might have had a particular type of skull. A blow with anything might have sunk it in like that.'

'No, sir, no sir.' The Scot sucked in air through his lips. 'That's clean against all the tenets of a very exact science. I will give you my opinion now. I'll not move from it in a court of law. It's a blunt weapon like a club or bortle that put out the light of yon poor fellow, and no amount of chaffering will make it into a stair-edge.'

Sir Daynes blasted this rebel in silence for a moment, but the Scot, seasoned to the attacks of many a defence counsel, was no apt subject for brow-beating. The baronet turned his attack on the imbecile Somerhayes.

'I suppose you've got something tangible to support this—this flimsy piece of medical evidence?'

Somerhayes silently shook his head.

'No idea who'd want to do it—no evidence about how it was done?'

'Nothing, Daynes, I'm afraid. Naturally I conducted a brief inquiry among the inmates of this establishment, but nothing relevant has come to light. As far as I can discover the Lieutenant was very popular with my household, including the domestic staff. I, personally, found his society refreshing, and he was a great favourite with the *tapissiers* and our *chef d' atelier*. I am unable to imagine any motive whatever for his death.'

'Hah!' exclaimed Sir Daynes triumphantly, 'and neither am I, Henry—neither am I. It's the most preposterous piece of twaddle I ever heard of. A man everyone likes takes a tumble down some stairs, and because he cracks his skull one way and not another everybody starts assuming there's been foul play. Blasted morbidity, that's what I call it. And you heard nothing—found nothing?'

'No, Daynes.'

'Not even a club or bortle?'—Sir Daynes gave the Scot a leer.

'Nothing of the sort has been discovered about the immediate scene of the tragedy. My butler-valet, Thomas, found the body when he was passing through the hall shortly after seven this morning. He immediately aroused me, and together we searched the hall and the galleries for any indication suggestive of what had occurred. We were both familiar with the precise disposition of the contents, but we could find nothing unusual or out of place.'

'Of course you damned-well couldn't! What would you expect to find after a feller falls downstairs?' Sir Daynes rubbed his hands with the air of one who was restoring rationality where madness had reigned. 'Let's be cool about this, Henry. We'd all been making merry last night. If that young feller wasn't used to hard liquor, it's ten to one he finished up a bit uncertain on his pins. Do you remember him drinking after we'd gone?'

'Yes,' assented Somerhayes, after a pause.

'Hah! And strong stuff at that?'

'The last drink we had was an '05 cognac.'

'There you are—what more do you want? A vintage cognac, on top of all other stuff we'd been putting away. The wonder is you didn't have to carry him to bed, not that he tripped over his feet at the top of the stairs. No, no, Somerhayes, I appreciate your anxiety about this. You've tackled the business like a good feller and a conscientious magistrate. But I assure you you're making too much of it. The shock of the thing has unsettled you, man. Now I'll just get an ambulance along and give the Coroner a tinkle, and we'll try to get this affair out of our minds. . . .'

Sir Daynes came to a halt, his eye falling on Gently. The forgotten Central Office man had apparently been doing some exploring, for he was now in the act of descending the great marble stairway. He looked woodenly at the baronet and then at Somerhayes, and Sir Daynes, who knew his Gently, felt a sudden uneasiness creep over him.

'This hall . . . is it cleaned out often?'

For some reason, a pin might have been heard to drop.

'Not at this time of the year.' Somerhayes' voice sounded flatter than ever. 'In summer when the visitors come it is cleaned several times a week, but now, perhaps not more than once a fortnight.'

'Would it have been last cleaned recently?'

'Yes, I think two days ago, in preparation for Christmas.'

Gently nodded his mandarin nod. He seemed quite unaware of the pregnant silence.

'So that if, out of six objects in the hall, five had a thin layer of dust and one had not, you would say that that one had been wiped at some time less than two days ago?'

Somerhayes' head slowly sank in acknowledgement.

'Damn it, man, what *is* all this?' erupted Sir Daynes fiercely. 'What the devil six objects are you talking about?'

Gently pointed up the stairway. Seven pairs of eyes followed his outstretched finger. On two oval panels, hung on each side of the marble doorway, were displayed six antique japanned-and-gilt truncheons.

'It's the lowest one on the left-hand side . . . do you think we might have it sent to the lab.?'

'Blast you, Gently!' roared Sir Daynes, 'I thought I asked you to keep out of this business?'

Gently hunched his shoulders and looked down at the sprawling figure at the foot of the stairs.

'There was somebody else who asked me to keep in,' he replied expressionlessly.

CHAPTER FOUR

DOCTOR SHIEL estimated the time of death at between one and three a.m. The ambulance had arrived and departed, Earle's belongings had been collected and examined by curious policemen. The best part of them were comprised by a pile of variously-shaped packages wrapped in silver foil and tied up with gold tinsel . . . each one was labelled, and it was a nice legal point whether the labels did or did not have the force of a last will and testament. Sir Daynes, with the air of one gripping a nettle, had phoned Earle's unit at Sculton and conservatively reported the details of the Lieutenant's demise.

'That'll mean trouble before we're very much older,' he forecast gloomily as he pressed down the receiver.

They had returned to the Manor for lunch, which was, of course, dinner; but the flavour had gone out of the festivities for that day. Sir Daynes was like a bear with a sore head. Even now he was unwilling to relinquish the comfortable theory of accidental death—surely that was a bad enough condiment for the turkey, without invoking the ultimate in misfortunes.

'I suppose that damned truncheon of yours clinches the matter,' he grumbled over his pudding. 'No other reason why it should be wiped . . . people don't go around wiping odd truncheons.'

'We'll know when we get the lab. report.' Gently was no more in love with life than his host.

'Could have been something else . . . some fool using it to poke the fire, or something. Or what about the feller himself? It's shaped like a baseball bat. Might have taken a swing or two with it, just to see how it was balanced. . . .'

'Daynes,' sighed his spouse, 'you'll almost certainly get indigestion. Why don't you let Inspector Dyson get on with it, and stop fretting like a broody hen?'

They were smoking cigars when the lab. got through. Sir Daynes was in the hall almost before the phone began ringing.

'Well—that's settled that! The lab. confirms it was the weapon. Among other things it has his brilliantine on it, and some impacted human skin.'

'There weren't any prints?'

'No—wiped off clean.'

'Someone didn't panic after the body went down the stairs. . . .'

'I think this is *horrid*,' exclaimed Lady Broke reprovingly. 'Daynes, I really will not have you discussing homicide in my lounge.'

'All right, m'dear!' Sir Daynes found a smile for her. 'Come on Gently, let's get back. Dyson is waiting the interrogations for us.'

The Place seemed as empty and as frigid as a gigantic sepulchre on that grey afternoon. Except for the constable, reinstalled outside the door, and the

servant who led them through the interminable dust-
sheeted rooms, they met nobody until they arrived at
the little blue drawing-room in the north-east wing.
Here Inspector Dyson was impatiently warming his
posterior at a newly-lit fire, and two constables stood
gleaning what they could, one on either side of him.

'Hah!' said Sir Daynes, by way of inspiring the atmosphere with his presence. The monosyllable had its
effect. A reluctant Dyson unbonneted the hearth,
which was immediately reinvested by the shameless
baronet. The two constables shrank yet further away
from the centre of comfort, and their places were
taken by Dyson and Gently.

'Hah!' repeated Sir Daynes with satisfaction. 'Don't
know how they got on in the eighteenth century, but
this blasted great barn has been an ice-house ever
since I can remember. Must have bred 'em tougher in
those days, Dyson. Must have had circulations like
double-action pumps. No wonder the confounded females wore eighteen petticoats, eh, eh?'

Dyson essayed a polite laugh, and Sir Daynes
rubbed his hands genially.

'Well now, about this business. You've had the lab.
report, have you?'

'Yes sir. It came half an hour ago.'

'What are your ideas, man? I suppose you've got
some?'

Dyson looked uncomfortable, as though he were a
bit low in that department.

'We've been all round the outside of the house, sir,
just in case there'd been a break-in. And Lord Somerhayes and some of his staff checked through the inside to see if anything was disturbed or missing.'

'Did y'get any results?'

'No sir.'

'Pity, Dyson.'

'Looks like an inside job, sir.'

'You don't have to blasted-well rub it in, Dyson.'

Sir Daynes knitted his brows, which were splendidly adapted to the purpose, and swayed forward slightly to adjust matters in his rear.

'And you've got some ideas?'

'Er . . . nothing concrete, sir.'

'You mean you *haven't* got any?'

'At this stage, sir, I thought it best to keep an open mind. . . .'

Sir Daynes grunted meaningfully, but refrained from a sarcasm which had obviously occurred to him. 'Well, let's get on with it,' he said. 'Ask Lord Somerhayes to come in.'

A constable was dispatched, and returned shortly to usher in the nobleman. Somerhayes looked more collected than he had done in the morning. The ghostly paleness had left his high-boned cheeks, there was some colour in his lips, a certain firmness, when he spoke, had replaced the near-hysteria-sounding flatness of his voice. He looked quickly around him on entering, and seeing Gently, gave him a fey little smile. Gently returned it with a solemn nod.

'Haven't interrupted your dinner, man, have we?' enquired Sir Daynes with concern.

'No, thank you, Daynes. I have had very little appetite for it.'

'Mistake, man, mistake. Should keep up your strength, y'know.'

Somerhayes made no reply, but took his seat in the

chair which had been set facing the table impressed
for the business of taking statements. Dyson took his
place opposite, his short-hand constable beside him:
Sir Daynes and Gently remained standing, the former
shifting over a bit to give Gently a fairer look at the
fire.

'Your full name, sir?'

'Henry Ainslie Charles Feverell, sixth Baron
Somerhayes.'

'Of Merely Place in the county of Northshire, sir?'

'Yes . . . Magistrate of that county.'

Why was he looking at Gently while he gave these
details, as though they constituted a wistful joke?

'We would like you to tell us, sir, what you know
about the deceased, and how he came to be staying at
Merely Place.'

Somerhayes crossed his legs with deliberation and
addressed himself to the task. He had nothing significant to tell them, but he gave it in precise detail. The
deceased had been introduced to him in the tapestry
workshop six weeks previously. He had been invited
there by Mr. Brass, following a lecture given by Mr.
Brass at the American Air Force base at Sculton. According to the deceased's account of himself, he was
the only son of a newspaper proprietor in the town of
Carpetville, Missouri, U.S.A., and his age was twenty-
three. He had had artistic training and was enthusiastically interested in the tapestry workshop. He had
subsequently paid a number of visits during which he
had taken weaving lessons from Mr. Brass, who had
been very favourably impressed by his pupil's ability,
and his general popularity had led Somerhayes to in-

vite the young man to spend his Christmas leave at the Place.

'He was a complete stranger to all the residents, sir, as far as you know?'

'A complete stranger.'

'None of the residents or staff are American, sir, or to your knowledge have been to that country?'

'None of them are American, and I would be surprised to learn that any of them except myself had been to America.'

'When were you in the States, Henry?' interrupted Sir Daynes in surprise. 'Thought you were attached to the Paris Embassy when you were in the Diplomatic Service?'

'I was there as a very young man,' agreed Somerhayes. 'But that was before the outbreak of war. During the war, as you know, I worked in the Foreign Office. It was while I was there that I had occasion to visit the United States.'

'And of course . . . never had anything to do with this feller or his family?' Sir Daynes sounded embarrassed at having to put such a tendentious question.

'I did not have that pleasure.'

'Of course not . . . too busy, eh? Didn't get around much.'

'I made a few excursions in the neighbourhood of Washington, but my acquaintance was confined to members of the Embassy and their families and friends. I had no opportunity to visit the State of Missouri.'

'Naturally . . . understand! Just have to get these things straight, y'know. Go on with what you were telling us, Henry . . . feller obviously a complete stranger.'

Sir Daynes relapsed into some throat-clearing and Somerhayes, unmoved, proceeded to relate the events leading up to the tragedy. He had sent his car to pick up Earle at Merely Halt on the evening of the twenty-third. The young man had arrived at some time after eleven, when the rest of the household had retired. Somerhayes had ordered him some supper and chatted with him while he ate it. He had been in high spirits, talking gaily of his experiences in London and of a certain 'amusing old buffer'—here Somerhayes' strange little smile again found Gently—who had travelled down with him. They had retired together to the north-east wing, where Somerhayes had given him a room in his own suite. In the morning Earle's high spirits had continued. He had begun the day by going round with a piece of mistletoe and kissing, it was understood, every female member of the household, including the housekeeper, who was fifty-nine. Later on he had gone to the workshop in the company of Mrs. Page and Mr. Brass, and had made a start at setting-up a low-warp machine on which he was purposing to weave a cartoon, or pattern, of his own design. During the afternoon he had accompanied Mrs. Page on a walk through the park to the folly, and during the evening he had made one of a party in the north-east wing, which was in communal use during the holiday.

'He was full enough of horse-play then, as I can testify,' grunted Sir Daynes. 'Young devil led me a caper or two.'

After Sir Daynes had left with Lady Broke and

Gently, Earle had wanted to continue with the fun. In view of the morrow, however, the party broke up shortly after midnight. The *tapissiers* had retired to their quarters in the south-east wing, which adjoined the workshop, Mr. Brass to his rooms in the south-west wing, and shortly afterwards, Mrs. Page to the suite she occupied in the north-west wing.

'So that for a short time there were yourself, Earle and Mrs. Page alone in the . . . where was it?' murmured Gently from his corner of the hearth.

Somerhayes paused directly in his statement. 'The Yellow drawing-room, Mr. Gently. Yes, that is perfectly correct, though the three of us were together for only a few minutes while my cousin finished some Sauternes she was drinking.'

'Would you remember the conversation?'

'I'm not certain that I would. I believe Lieutenant Earle was describing to us the advantages of a visit to Missouri, which he would have liked to have persuaded us to make. But as I said, my cousin did not remain with us longer than it took her to finish her drink.'

'After which Lieutenant Earle and yourself were left together?'

Somerhayes looked Gently straight in the eyes.

'Yes,' he said.

They had sat by the dying fire until Somerhayes had been called away by Thomas, his butler-valet, with some question about the laying-out of presents in the wing breakfast-room. When he returned to the Yellow drawing-room Earle was still there, and they had had a night-cap together. Then Earle had gone up to his room, at about one a.m., and Somerhayes had followed him ten minutes later, after giving some final instructions to Thomas.

'Was Thomas there, sir, when the deceased retired?' enquired Dyson quickly.

Somerhayes shook his head. 'Thomas was busy in the breakfast-room. I returned to him there after seeing Lieutenant Earle go up. As you probably know, in this wing one passes the stairs to the first floor on the way from the Yellow drawing-room to the breakfast-room.'

'And you left Thomas in the breakfast-room when you retired, sir?'

'Yes. I left him putting out the silver.'

Dyson nobly restrained himself from jumping down his distinguished informant's throat, but it was with a visible effort.

'Like that, sir, you were the last person to see him alive?' he suggested carefully.

'I was,' replied Somerhayes flatly, without the suspicion of an evasion.

'Hrrmp, hrrmp!' interrupted Sir Daynes. 'Apart from the criminal, of course, apart from the criminal. Suppose the young feller did go up to his room, Somerhayes? Bed wasn't slept in, y'know.'

'I cannot be positive, Sir Daynes. He expressed the intention, and I last saw him ascending the stairs.'

'Didn't you hear him moving about when you went up? Room only one away from yours, eh? Passed your door when he was on his way out of the wing?'

Somerhayes did not reply immediately. His expression a blank, he seemed to be running over in his mind every minute detail of the night before.

'No,' he said at last. 'I can be of no help to you on

that point. I heard nothing from his room when I went up, nor later when I was in bed. Being tired, I went to sleep quickly, and I remembered nothing more until I was wakened by Thomas at ten minutes past seven.'

'Feller might never have gone to his room, then?'

'As you say, Daynes, he might not.'

There was a small commotion by the hearth as Gently searched the pocket of his ulster and produced a crumpled pamphlet. It was a visitor's guide to the Place, of which a small pile still lay on a side-table in the great hall.

'If you don't mind . . . I'd like to get these premises clear in my brain.'

He opened the guide on the table and turned the pages with clumsy fingers. On the verso of the cover was printed a plan of the state apartments, in shape a large rectangle, its width two-thirds its length. At each corner were four smaller rectangles representing the wings. They were connected to the central block by narrow ante-rooms or galleries. In the centre of the state apartments, facing east, was the great hall, with galleries running round its three inner walls. From the inner end of the hall, at almost the exact centre of the block, the flight of marble stairs descended from the gallery-level.

'All this isn't used at all . . . it just connects the four wings?'

Gently poked at the enormous central block, which dwarfed its four appendages.

Somerhayes smiled bleakly. 'It was not built for utility, Mr. Gently. The state apartments were designed to house visiting royalty and the first Baron's

collection of pictures and antiques. In a more
spacious age they were certainly in frequent use, but
I believe there is no record of the family having inhabited other than the wings. To-day, I'm afraid, the
state apartments are no more than a museum which
in summer we open to the public. At other times they
are merely an insuperable inconvenience to the poor
inhabitants.'

'Going round the clock . . . who lives where?'

'Going round the clock we have first the south-east
wing, in which the *tapissiers* and the outdoor staff
have their quarters—it has entry, you see, into the
coach-houses and stabling, part of which has been
turned into the tapestry workshop. Next at that end
is the south-west wing where Mr. Brass has rooms,
and above him the indoor staff. In that wing are also
the kitchens. Coming to this end we have, first, the
north-west wing, which is my cousin's sacred domain,
and second the north-east wing, in which we are now,
and which Thomas and myself inhabit. In the usual
way all meals are taken in the kitchen wing, but it
was decided that over Christmas my own suite would
be used, and so the Yellow drawing-room here was
the scene of last night's party. I trust you can find
your way about now, Mr. Gently?'

Gently nodded broodingly. He placed a stubby finger on the top of the great stairs.

'That's about equidistant from each of the four
wings.'

'The landing of the marble stairs, is, I believe the
geometric centre of the house.'

'In fact it's the logical place for a rendezvous . . .
don't you think?'

Somerhayes said nothing, but his eyes never left Gently's face.

'We've got to ask ourselves why he went there —at that time of night. It isn't just around the corner . . . see here, there's four or five rooms to go through after you've left this wing, not to mention the gallery on the north side of the hall. What was he after, unless he'd arranged to meet someone?'

Somerhayes shook his head slowly. 'I can suggest no reason. . . .'

'And what was the object of the meeting, which was presumably clandestine?'

Again the head shook, unhurriedly but with determination.

'Gad Gently, you've got something there,' broke in Sir Daynes. 'If the feller went to meet someone, must have been clandestine. D'you think he was a bad 'un, and this tapestry fal-de-lal was just a blind?'

'Be a good way of getting in, sir,' put in Dyson with interest.

'Damn it, yes—confounded clever. And not above some of the johnnies we've had to deal with.'

It was Gently's head that was shaking now. 'He comes from a U.S. camp, you know. . . .'

'That's just the point, man,' exclaimed Sir Daynes. 'Who's going to check his credentials, when he turns up at an Air Force lecture? Feller's genuine—take him at his face value—and all the time he's a crook, infiltrating his way into a country house. It's been done before, I tell you. There's no end to the tricks these johnnies get up to.'

'But surely they'd know their own officers at the camp?'

'Not necessarily—not at Sculton. Place is a staging-post, men in and out the whole time. And the whole business fits in . . . you've got a motive there to play with. Feller lets his accomplice into the house, say,—they quarrel about the division of the loot—accomplice fetches him one with the truncheon, and clears off sharp without touching anything. There you are, man, in a nutshell. Answer to the whole confounded mystery.'

Gently shrugged his bulky shoulders. 'Just one minor objection. Did they happen to know who you were talking about when you phoned Sculton Camp this morning . . . ?'

Sir Daynes gave him the look he usually reserved for defaulting constables. . . .

They could get little more out of Somerhayes. For the benefit of the record he repeated his description of the finding of the body, of his suspicion about the injury, of the search he had made with Thomas, and the subsequent phoning of the police and Sir Daynes. And all the time Gently had the curious impression that he had been constituted as some sort of special audience, that he was a gallery to whom Somerhayes was playing. But why? And with what object?—the circumstances remained a mystery. Somerhayes' last look, like his first, was an unclassifiable smile aimed at the man from the Central Office.

'Hmp!' grunted Sir Daynes, as the door closed behind his lordship. 'What do you make of it all, Gently, what do you make of it? Can't say I like the way things are shaping—damn' feller Somerhayes doesn't seem to realize his position.'

'He was the last person to——' Dyson was beginning

complacently, but he discreetly ended there as he caught the expression on the baronet's face.

'Confound the man!' Sir Daynes turned to stare gloomily into the fire. 'What a blasted kettle of fish to turn up on a Christmas Day, eh? I feel like a drink . . . I feel like some of that '05 cognac.'

CHAPTER FIVE

LESLIE BRASS, dressed in green Harris tweed with a red line, seemed to bring a current of vitality with him into the room which Somerhayes had chilled and enervated. One only had to catch a glimpse of his strong features with their Semitic nose and twinkling green eyes to be impressed by a feeling of warmth and energy—the ginger beard suited Brass; it seemed to grow out of his personality like an overplus of good spirits. When he sat down, the chair creaked under his massive but boyish frame.

'Leslie Edward Brass, thirty-seven, artist—this isn't the first time I've given the police my particulars!—late of Kensington, W.8, now of Merely Place, Northshire—servant's wing, if you want to be precise.'

Nothing was going to make this serious for Brass. He grinned irreverently at the whole of the set-up. Policemen might impress the bourgeois, but from Brass they just bounced off—his piratical spirits surrounded him like an envelope of indiarubber.

'What do you want to know—if I did for our young friend?'

Dyson tried to quell him with a might-take-you-at-your-word look, but it was a pure waste of talent.

'We'd like you to tell us what you know of the deceased, Mr. Brass, and everything you can remember about last night.'

'I can tell you straight away that I've got nothing for you.'

'We'd like it in the form of a statement, sir, *if* you don't mind.'

Brass didn't mind. He was a born raconteur. Without further prompting, he launched into a racy account of his meeting with Earle at the Sculton lecture, of his amusement at the young man's gaucherie and enthusiasm, of the American's impact on the small, closed world of the Place.

'My trained seals didn't know what to make of him at first—he spent half his time chasing the females, and the other half telling us how to weave tapestry. Lucky for him he was a natural charm-boy. We could have hated his guts if he hadn't been. But he soon found out he didn't know much, and he never minded admitting it. Had 'em all eating from his hand, he did, by the time he'd spent a couple of days with us. And as I've said before, many a time, he had some real, hard talent in him. If I could have kept him with me a few years the name of Earle would have meant something in the dove-cotes. But he wouldn't have stopped over here, so it didn't signify. He'd got some wild ideas about setting up a tapestry workshop in the States, as though you could learn tapestry in five minutes—then he'd got another idea about transplanting me to Carpetville, Missouri. The kid was full of notions. It's a pity they've gone to pot.'

'Feller never had a quarrel with any of the

whady'-callems—*tapissiers*?' enquired Sir Daynes from over his commandeered cognac.

Brass made a gesture with his white, conical fingers.

'You couldn't quarrel with a kid like that. He had a born sweetness of disposition. You could rib the lights out of him—I often did—and he'd never dream of taking offence. As far as he was concerned, it was a world without malice. You could club his feelings as somebody clubbed his head, and he would just think it one hell of a lark.'

'Mmn.' Sir Daynes didn't seem to favour the parallel. 'You can't suggest anyone who might have had it in for him?'

'Not a soul, I'd say. Unless it was Hugh Johnson.'

'Johnson? Who's he?'

'A Welsh griffin we've got in our outfit. But don't make a mistake—Johnson wouldn't have brained the kid. He was just a bit sore because Earle put his nose out of joint. Johnson's a fine designer, and I've been grooming him for stardom. Then Earle came along and I spent a lot of time on him, as a result of which dear Hugh decided to be huffy.'

Sir Daynes was obviously interested. His knitted brow betrayed the fact. 'Suppose this Welshman didn't threaten him—nothing of that sort?'

'Good heavens, no! You mustn't start suspecting our Hugh.'

'But he'd got it in for him?'

'In the mildest possible way.'

'Hmn,' said Sir Daynes, and visibly made a note.

Brass continued his statement, which as far as it went corroborated that of Somerhayes. When the party broke up he had left Earle with Somerhayes and Mrs. Page. He had gone to his rooms at the other corner of the huge establishment, and as far as he could testify, a quiet and *heilige* night was had by all. He was wakened by Thomas in the morning at between twenty and a quarter to eight. He found Somerhayes in the hall, about to cover the body with a blanket.

'Did you form any impression of his . . . um . . . state of mind at the time?'

The room had warmed up, and Gently had left the hearth for a seat by the deep, stone-framed window.

'State of mind. . . .' Brass swung around to him, a return of last night's cynicism in his lively eye. 'Well, he was in a bad state of shock, of course. There isn't much toughness about his Lordship. He was as white as a sheet and as quiet as a dolmen. He showed me the bash, asked me if I knew anything, and then left me on guard while he ghosted off to tinkle you blokes.'

'Would you say that his Lordship was very fond of the deceased?'

Brass gave a little chuckle. 'He wasn't one of his *âmes intimes*, if you know what I mean. But he was fond enough of him, just as we all were. Being American had something to do with it.'

'How do you mean, Mr. Brass?'

'Why, his Lordship is one of those types who find something mystical in the idea of America—it's a symbol, you understand, it stands for spiritual youth and virility. Over here we're bankrupt and done for. We've been at it too long, we're suffering from hardened arteries. I daresay his Lordship could feel the same way about Russia if his politics didn't prevent it.'

'Feller always had queer ideas,' grumbled Sir Daynes, still guarding the hearth. 'Turned Liberal when he was a young fool at Oxford—upset his father, I can tell you. Never been a Whig in the family since George the First.'

'And you think Earle's being American inclined his Lordship to favour him?' Gently persisted.

'Certain of it.' Brass waved his hand.

'It would not have been held against him, for instance, if he had been making overtures to his Lordship's cousin?'

'Janice?' Brass's eyebrows lifted in surprise. 'You're not going to tell me that the young heathen was making up to her?'

'It did occur to me, Mr. Brass.'

The artist guffawed his amusement. 'Good lord, what impressions people get. You don't know your young American, Inspector. You don't know Janice, either. Our little sex-delinquent exercised his charm on every frail, broad, and doll who came within yards of him—including the housekeeper, who is no Ninon. You're barking up the wrong tree there, Inspector.'

Gently shrugged. 'You could be right.'

'*En tout cas*, he wouldn't have got any change out of Janice. She's still carrying Des Page's torch. She's a Feverell too, you know—they take things to heart in that family. You can take my word for it that Janice P. is man-proof.'

Gently nodded indefinitely. 'But supposing his Lordship had formed a certain impression . . . his reactions would have been favourable?'

'On the surface, anyway, I don't see why not.'

'But under the surface, Mr. Brass?'

The artist made a wry face. 'Christ knows what goes on under the sixth Lord's surface! I don't know, and I'm not going to be led into hazarding guesses. I'm eating his salt, anyway. It doesn't become me to tell tales out of school.'

'This is homicide, you know. . . .'

'That's why it's dangerous to gossip.'

'Anything pertinent is not gossip.'

'Let's say I've got nothing pertinent, and call it a day.'

Gently shrugged again and turned to peer out at the advancing twilight. Sir Daynes made some noises which to the knowledgeable betokened dissatisfaction.

'You're not holding anything back, eh . . . mistaken sense of loyalty and that?'

'Damnation no! Didn't I tell you at the beginning of this session that I'd got nothing for you?'

'Just want to be sure, man . . . understand a thing like that.'

Brass departed as indeflatable as he had come, and Sir Daynes, wrenching himself from the matured and beautiful fire, joined Gently at the window. For a moment he stood there in silence, contemplating the dreary prospect, then he flashed a glance at the Central Office man which was the reverse of friendly.

'Confound it, Gently . . . lay off Somerhayes,' he mumbled, *sotto voce*. 'I can see what you're getting at . . . man and his pretty cousin. But it won't do, I tell you, and what's more I don't like it. Things look black enough now for the poor feller . . . and I'm damn' certain he's in the clear.'

Gently hunched himself deeper in the ulster, which
he hadn't taken off.

'I'm not getting at anything . . . I'm just following the ball,' he replied.

'Well, I don't like the way it's rolling.'

'I'm not sure I do, either. But one thing is certain
enough, if you follow it to the end . . . you'll come
to a point where a murderer's bludgeon struck an innocent head.'

Sir Daynes snorted. 'There's another thing certain.
I ought to blasted-well order you back to the Manor
to keep Gwen company! Hrmp, hrmp. I suppose it's
Mrs. Page you want to see in here next?'

An interesting tray had been brought in soon after
Brass was dismissed. It bore several bottles of varying
silhouettes, a selection of glasses, and some slices of
iced cake reposing on a napkinned salver. This
caused some awkwardness for Inspector Dyson, who
had a strong sense of duty; but a proper ruling from
Sir Daynes quickly relieved the situation, and soon
two constables, one Inspector, one Chief Inspector
and a Chief Constable were fortifying themselves
against the season and making good any gaps which
might have appeared since lunch-time. Within
bounds, it was a festive scene. The glamour was extended when permission was given to smoke, and Sir
Daynes distributed the high-calibre contents of his
cigar-case. One did not often see five policemen, two
of them in uniform, puffing Havanahs while they
solemnly partook of vintage port and mellowed
liqueurs, and some surprise was to be looked for in

the face of Mrs. Page when she appeared through the door. Sir Daynes hurried over to her and put a fatherly arm round her shoulders.

'Don't be alarmed, m'dear, don't be alarmed. Only keep you a few minutes, y'know . . . . Somerhayes just sent in a snifter to keep our spirits up.'

Mrs. Page smiled, but it seemed to Gently that it required an effort. There wasn't much colour in her transparent cheeks, and about her eyes, so like and yet so unlike her cousin's, ran the suspicion of two dark circles. She sat down boldly enough, however, and Dyson, hurriedly getting rid of his cigar, was put a little out of countenance.

'Like some sherry, m'dear . . . cherry brandy, perhaps?'

'No thank you, Sir Daynes. We have been drinking in the lounge.'

'Bad business, eh? Bad business! Impossible to imagine who'd want to do any harm to a likeable young feller like that.'

Mrs. Page bit her beautiful lips, and for a moment it looked as though she would burst into tears. The moment passed; she sat very upright. Sir Daynes, pulling up a chair, placed himself deliberately between her and Gently.

'Now just give the Inspector your full name and age and address, m'dear . . . that's the ticket. Be twenty-nine for some years yet, eh? Now all you have to do is to tell us what you know about the feller, and anything you can remember about what happened after he came here. . . .'

From the way she spoke it sounded as though she

had been rehearsing it. For all she could do, it would
come out in little rushes of pre-composed phrasing.
And the tenor of it was exactly what they had heard
before. With minor variations, it was the identical account given by Somerhayes and Brass. The artist had
talked scoffingly of him the day after the lecture had
been delivered. On the week-end following, driving a
rattle-trap Buick he had borrowed from a friend,
Earle had parked on the Place terrace and manfully
rung the front-door bell. He had made mixed impressions. The *tapissiers* were an absorbed and conser-
vative little community, and Earle, though he had
charm, had very little tact. But his enthusiasm was
genuine enough, and so, too, was his talent, and after
another visit or two the *tapissiers* had taken him to
their hearts. Somerhayes had shown a liking for him
from the outset.

'Must interrupt, m'dear, but what about a feller
called Hugh Johnson . . . what was his attitude to
Earle?'

'Johnson?' Mrs. Page hesitated awkwardly. 'Well,
he might have been the exception, I suppose. He's a
Welshman, you know . . . very clever and all that,
but rather . . . well, introspective, I suppose you'd
call it. He's apt to sulk a bit.'

'Nurse a grudge would he?'

'I don't think he would forget one in a hurry.'

'Sort of feller who might turn nasty?'

'I . . . wouldn't like to say that. He's quick, of
course, soon fires up and all that . . . and sullen—
that's the word for it. He broods over things for days.
But he can be a dear, too, when he likes.'

'Hah. And he took against Earle?'

'He was a little surly towards him. He felt that Earle had displaced him with Brass. To a certain extent that was true.'

'Complained about it, did he?'

'Oh no, Hugh was much too proud to complain. But he had some things to say about Americans being all talk, and cutting things like that. And he used to snub Earle unmercifully, which was a sheer waste of time . . . Earle being. . . .'

Mrs. Page broke off, and from the sinking movement of her head as well as the sudden rise in her voice, Gently judged that she was again struggling on the verge of tears.

'There, there,' mumbled Sir Daynes. 'Shocking affair, m'dear, shocking. Take your time. Got all day. Dyson, stub that confounded cigar-butt . . . smoke's getting in the lady's eyes.'

The head rose again, and after a pause Mrs. Page was ready to go on. Once more the short-hand constable's pencil commenced whisking down the page. They had been very much looking forward to having Earle with them at Christmas. At first there was some doubt as to whether he could get leave, but the easing of the current political tension had enabled the Sculton C.O. to grant one or two passes, Earle's amongst them. He had long planned his day of Christmas shopping in London. He had wanted Mrs. Page to accompany him, but she had been prevented from doing so by the necessity of clearing up the business-end of the workshop before the Christmas break.

On the morning after his arrival he had been at his

most exuberant; he had dominated the breakfast-table with his account of his visit to London, and directly afterwards had dragged Les and herself away to the workshop to help him set up the loom for his famous cartoon. After lunch he had wanted to stretch his limbs and look at the park. She had consented to walk with him as far as the folly, from which there was a striking prospect of the house and the lake, and on the way he had talked a great deal about his home in Missouri, and about his people, and about the sort of Christmas they would be spending there. He had also talked of a projected visit to Missouri which he was trying to persuade Les to make with him in the autumn, and which he wanted her to undertake also. His lively behaviour at the party Sir Daynes himself had been witness to. When the party broke up, the various members of it had retired in the order already vouched for, and she had first heard of the tragedy when her personal maid brought in the tea at eight o'clock.

'Fine,' exclaimed Sir Daynes at the end of the recital. 'That's all we wanted to know, m'dear, you've given us a perfect model of a statement. Wish everyone could be so precise, eh? Lots of people can't. But that's all we want to know, and you can run along now. . . .'

The words froze on the baronet's lips as he became aware of Gently looming up on his flank.

'Yes, Gently?' he demanded sharply.

'Just one small point. . . .'

Sir Daynes drew in his breath wickedly, but he could think of no good reason for applying a veto.

'Well?' he rapped.

'At the party last night . . . Mrs. Page, his Lordship and the deceased were alone for a short time. Could Mrs. Page oblige us with a description of the conversation which took place?'

'Confound it, man! Already had that from Somerhayes. Young feller was still carrying on about Missouri, wasn't he, m'dear?'

'Yes—he was.' Mrs Page was staring at Gently with something like fear in her large eyes.

'Mmn . . . and after that . . . when you were leaving, and the deceased accompanied you to the door?'

The eyes jumped open wide. 'My cousin didn't tell you that! I didn't—I——' She broke off, turning imploringly to Sir Daynes. 'He didn't accompany me to the door—I left him talking to my cousin. Ask him, Sir Daynes, he'll tell you that it's true!'

Nobody in the room could have mistaken the baronet's slightly delayed reaction. He weighed in quickly, but not quite quickly enough.

'—course it's true, m'dear—suggestion's downright preposterous!'

'You've only to ask my cousin——'

'Not necessary, m'dear. Take your word any day.'

'The Inspector is entirely mistaken.'

'The Inspector,' said Sir Daynes feelingly, 'has been a mistake all along—hrmp, hrmp! I mean, we're all human, m'dear, always have to allow a margin for error!'

Mrs. Page left the room hastily, and the baronet glared warningly, first at Dyson and then at Gently. By the latter he was met with a far-away smile, and the Central Office man's lips formed a word which only Sir Daynes could hear: '*Touché!*'

'What are we waiting for?' bawled Sir Daynes. 'Fetch in that feller Johnson, and let's see if we can't get a grip on this business!'

CHAPTER SIX

THE LIGHTS had been on all the afternoon; the atmosphere, grown mild and expansive, was pleasantly tinctured with the smoke of cigars. Before they had drawn the curtains patterns had appeared on the single panes, and the brightness of the fire corroborated this wintry phenomenon.

'Damned pond'll get frozen,' muttered Sir Daynes to Gently, forgetting his antagonism as he remembered their common addiction. 'Don't suppose you skate, do you? I can fix you up with a pair. Gwen likes to have her twiddle on the ice, but I'm not much of a skating man myself.'

'We can fish through a hole, perhaps. . . .'

'Ha, ha, not on this pond, m'boy. When the ice gets set it's sacred to Gwen. Woman would never forgive me if I started knocking holes in it.'

'You can fish more often than you can skate, I suppose.'

'That's the argument I've had used against me for the past thirty years.'

'There's more frost on the way, sir,' put in Dyson through his teeth. 'I heard the one o'clock news, sir. There's a cold airstream moving in from Siberia.'

'Blasted Russians again . . . stoke up that fire! D'you reckon the Cold War's a plot to make us use up our coal reserves?'

The fire was built up to its teeth by the time Johnson arrived. The Welshman gave it an appreciative glance, as though the rigours of a trip through the state apartments had immediately preceded his entry. He was a man of medium height, and his build was that of a boxer. He had broad, slightly rounded shoulders tapering quickly to narrow hips, his arms were long in proportion to his height, and his hands were bony and hard-looking. His head, of which the skull belonged to the long, narrow variety, sat closely on his shoulders; his hair was dark, his eyes darker, and there was a livid blue tattoo-mark on his weathered-looking forehead.

'Hugh Llewellyn Johnson, thirty-eight, and my family lives at Merthyr.'

'You are a tapestry-weaver, Mr. Johnson?'

'Aye, that I am, though I was ten years in the mines.'

'That's where you got that birth-mark, eh?' interpolated Sir Daynes, with suspicious casualness.

'Oh yes, I did—you can always tell a miner. I got that one in Gwrw Pit in 'forty.'

'Hit on the head, eh?'

'Man, I was bloody-well buried—did you never hear of the Gwrw? Two days we were down there, and never heard a sound. The dead men were lying with us. There's some who lies there yet.'

'Hmn. Nasty experience, what?'

'It's one I won't forget.'

'Sort of thing to give you dreams, and that?'

'Sometimes I dream I'm down there still, and wake up tearing the clothes off my limbs.'

Sir Daynes rubbed his hands with a sort of grisly satisfaction, and leaned back comfortably in his chair.

'Suppose you never get black-outs—that sort of thing?'

The ex-miner shook his head.

'Ah well . . . get on with your statement, man. Tell the Inspector what you know about the deceased.'

Johnson's statement followed the now-familiar pattern in its early stages. He had been working at his loom when Earle had been brought into the workshop for the first time. Johnson, who was an artist as well as a weaver, was at work on a tapestry from his own cartoon picturing the Glasllyn and Y Wyddfa, and Earle, with his customary tactlessness, had taken it upon himself to assure Johnson that the colour-values were incorrect. Johnson had thereupon catechized Earle on his knowledge of colour-values, more especially as applied to tapestry and the uncertain art of dyeing. Earle had been obliged to admit his profound ignorance, at least touching the two latter.

'Took him down a peg, did you?' inquired the subtle Sir Daynes.

'Oh yes, a good peg or two. He knew nothing whateffer of dyeing and sunlight tests.'

'Sent him off with a flea in his ear, eh?'

'Well no, not exactly, he wasn't a man you could handle like that. But I read him a good sermon, that I'll warrant you. By the time I had done he knew a good deal more about tapestry than when I had started.'

Nevertheless, Earle had got off on the wrong foot with Johnson. It was easy to see that the Welshman found it difficult to forgive the reckless strictures on his expert art. When he found himself being neglected by Brass, till then his constant admirer and teacher, the grudge was already in being to be fanned into active dislike.

'I don't mind admitting I could neffer get on with the man. Americans within reason, I say, but this one was a plain nuisance about the place. He was always upsetting the womenfolk, man, there wasn't half of the work done when he was around. And he had no respect for his betters at all. You would think he was a Royal Tudor at least, the way he carried on.'

'Not so big, either, but you could have put him down, eh?'

'Do you doubt it, man, when I have been in the ring with Tommy Farr himself, down there in Tony-pandy?'

'Boxing man, are you, Johnson?'

'Good gracious yess—I have my cups to prove it. Five years I was the Area Middleweight Champion, and not far past it now. I have fought the best, I tell you. There are many good men with the mark of Hugh Johnson's glove on their jaw.'

'Wonder you didn't clip this Yank one.'

'I have wondered myself too, before to-day. But you could never get him fighting, man, that was the whole trouble. You could say what you like to him, it would never get him mad. Some men are made that way. They haven't got the wickedness to play on. I tell you, it would have been like meat and drink to me sometimes to see that young man with my blood in his eye!'

Sir Daynes angled a bit further, but there were no fish to be caught, so he handed the questioning back to Dyson.

Johnson, at all events, hadn't received the news of Earle's Christmas visit with enthusiasm. Had he known in time, he would have arranged to spend his Christmas in his home town, along with a married sister. But the uncertainty had prevented that. Christmas leave had been cancelled at Sculton, and was only restored at the last moment. Sullenly, the Welshman had brooded over the prospect of what he considered to be a spoiled Christmas.

'You will say I was no true Christian to take against the man that way, and after what has happened, now, I may be sorry that I did. But God help us, man, there are some people who just get in our bowels and blood—Christian it may not be, but by St. David, it is human!'

Earle had arrived, and Johnson's worst fears were realized. The young American was in his most bumptious and obnoxious mood. Moreover, he had been granted a sort of general license by the rest of the household. They were all in a tale to worship Earle, and, as a natural consequence, to condemn the surly Welshman. Johnson had retired into his shell. He had always felt a little alien in this Saesneg establishment, and now circumstances had taken a turn which seemed to cut him off entirely. Dourly he accepted the part forced upon him. He was an outsider—very well. He would play an outsider's role. Without looking for trouble—was it not the season of goodwill?—he would make them feel the injustice of their attitude towards him, and the folly of abasing themselves to this American clown. Merely Place had deserved its Diogenes, and it should have one.

The Welshman broke off, his dark eyes darting fiercely from one to the other of them.

'And now I have it in mind to tell you the whole truth about what I saw after the party last night. At first I was not certain. A big thing it is, deciding if it is best to tell the police something which may cause trouble. But a crime has been done, a wicked, evil crime, and the guilt must lie where it lies though the devil himself cries Silence. So now I will tell you.'

Sir Daynes made sounds as though to applaud these upright sentiments, and Johnson, drawing his chair closer to the table, continued:

'The bile is a bad thing for a man's stomach, look you, and strong wine is no good fellow for it. When I got to my room after the party last night I could not sleep no more than fly, so, after pacing my room for some time, I had a mind to go to the library and fetch myself a book.'

'Eh?' ejaculated Sir Daynes, sitting up very straight. 'What library, man? What time was this?'

'As to the time, I do not know precisely, but the library is the one in the state drawing-room, which is handy for our wing.'

'The state drawing-room!' Sir Daynes was making noble efforts to establish a mental picture of the lay-out of the state apartments. 'But wait a minute, man—state drawing-room. Hasn't that got a door to the gallery in the great hall?'

'It has indeed. It gives straight on to it.'

'And you—you're admitting you went there, some time after the party last night?'

'A good hour after—past one o'clock, I'd say.'

Sir Daynes stared at the ex-miner, a curious glint in his eye. 'Go on,' he said, 'go on, Johnson.'

'Well as I stood there, looking through the bookcase, I thought I heard some voices in the hall. Not loud, you understand, but not soft either. It sounded like two people in an argument, and now and then they'd let their voices rise a little.'

'Whose voices were they, man?'

'I could not say. One of them was a woman.'

'A woman!'—Sir Daynes jerked his head back. 'Well . . . go on.'

'The voices stopped. I slipped out to the gallery. They have a light there in the hall, a single bulb, and I could just make out the gallery stretching back there, like a great horse-shoe. At first there was nothing to see, but then I heard a step over by the stairs, and out of the big marble doorway came the figure of a woman—in a hurry she was—and disappeared towards the other side of the house. After that it was all quiet, and I went back to my room. And that is the whole truth, God help me, of what I saw after last night's party.'

The expressions which passed over Sir Daynes' face during the latter part of this recital were worth the study of an actor. First his eyes opened wide and his jaw imperceptibly sank. Then a flush spread over his features, and the jaw squared up. Finally his eyes narrowed to two steely points, and his lips, pressed together, pouted aggressively outwards.

'And the woman?' he barked.

'I could not swear to her at all.'

'Yet you saw her, you say?'

'Oh yess, make no doubt of that.'

'But you don't know who she was?'

'No, I could not tell her from Eve. How could I, man, in that light, and from the far end of the gallery?'

'You could see she was a woman.'

'That is another thing altogether.'

'I put it to you that you're lying, Johnson.'

'And I tell you, man, that I am not a liar!'

There was a forward movement on the part of one constable as the fiery Welshman smashed his fist down on the table, while Sir Daynes, for his part, looked no less likely to keep the peace. For a moment they glared at each other like two enraged terriers.

'You admit you were in the gallery?' snarled Sir Daynes.

'Have I not said I was?'

'And at the crucial time?'

'At the time I have given in my statement.'

'And that was the time when the crime was committed.'

'Oh no it was *not*, for I can bear testimony.'

'And your damned testimony may put you in dock, my man, that's all the value *it's* likely to have! Why didn't you see the body?'

'Because there was no body to see.'

'And you didn't hear it, eh, tumbling down those stairs?'

'No more than you did, tucked up in your precious Manor House.'

'Don't answer the Chief Constable back,' yapped Dyson, feeling it was time he got a word in.

'Man,' retorted Johnson, thrusting his face towards the Inspector, 'take that police-badge out of your lapel for a moment, and I'll give you some free bloody dental treatment!'

It was a deplorable state of affairs. The official atmosphere had deteriorated to a point approaching zero. It was perhaps as well that at this juncture a bulky figure rose from a seat by the window and quietly joined itself to the end of the conference table.

'About that person you saw . . .' murmured Gently, spreading out his guide.

Three people, for three different reasons, restrained a *cri-de-cœur* which sprang automatically to the tips of their tongues. . . .

'I suppose you're happy, Gently,' observed Sir Daynes sourly, what time the room was again free of belligerent Welshmen. 'You wanted to drag Janice into this, and you've confounded-well succeeded. On the face of it, we'll have to ask her what she's got to say about the business.'

Gently's shoulders heaved expressionlessly. 'It might have been anyone. . . .'

'Might have been—but wasn't, eh? That's what you were going to say. And if we're to pay any attention to that damned concussed miner with his grudges and violence——!' Sir Daynes gave one of his finance-committee snorts. 'But have it your own way. Drag out all the dirty linen. We'll have Janice and Henry through the mill a dozen times if necessary—before we send that Johnson feller up with an indictment.'

'He's my first choice, sir,' assented Dyson with a touch of animosity in his tone. 'I couldn't begin to see my way into this case before we questioned *him*.'

'Hah, smelt him from the first!' Sir Daynes turned to his Inspector fondly. 'Always look for the grudge-bearer, Dyson, and you'll never go far wrong. Who would want to bash the feller? Answer, Johnson. Who was the type to do it? Answer, Johnson. Who had the opportunity? Answer, Johnson. And between you and me, Dyson, we've got our man, only there are a few loose ends about which the best detectives don't leave showing!'

Gently fished around in the pockets of his waistcoat and, after several failures, brought up a solitary, shop-soiled peppermint cream. 'We still don't know why Earle was out there in the hall,' he said. 'Until we do know we can't be certain of anything. The reason may be quite incidental, in which case Johnson may very well have taken an opportunity to level some scores . . . though, at the same time. . . .'

'Well, man?' demanded Sir Daynes impatiently.

'. . . can you honestly see Johnson bludgeoning Earle from behind?'

Sir Daynes rumbled and grumbled, but he was obliged to admit that he couldn't. On all other points the ex-miner added up to the required specifications, on this one he was a miserable failure.

'No.' Gently revolved the peppermint cream on his thumb. 'Johnson simply isn't the type to strike a cowardly blow in the dark. He's a boxer, a fighting man. His method of settling scores is to pick a quarrel and throw some punches. But setting that aside . . . he might have been tempted . . . if the reason for

Earle's being in the hall was not incidental, it may have been contrived by someone other than Johnson and until we know why or by whom it came about we shall be groping in the dark.'

'You mean we should disprove his statement about seeing a woman?' enquired Sir Daynes, with a little more favour.

'Possibly . . . it would have a negative value.'

'Show the feller is a liar, eh?'

'It wouldn't be less useful to show that he was not.'

Sir Daynes frowned at the peppermint cream, the revolutions of which seemed to fascinate him. 'I don't like it,' he said at last. 'Tell you straight, I think it'll stir up a stink to no purpose. We've got the feller's statement—he was in the hall at the time of the murder. What the devil does it matter *why* Earle came there, when the blasted fact is that he *did*?'

Gently raised the peppermint cream like a beacon between them. 'It could just be that Johnson is telling the truth . . .' he said.

For a moment longer Sir Daynes stared at the erected sweetmeat, then he swore under his breath and rapped an order to the apprehensive constable. Dyson began to say something, but the baronet shut him up with a look. The peppermint cream, flipped expertly, went to join its multitudinous predecessors.

'Hah, m'dear,' whinnied Sir Daynes, as Mrs. Page made her reappearance. 'Little point has come up—nothing important, answer it in a minute. Chief Inspector here wants to know something—think I'll let him pop the question. Know what you'll say already, but we have to show chapter and verse.'

Mrs. Page flickered a smile at him, but it came and went with pitiful rapidity. She was trembling as she sat down, her beautiful fingers moved restlessly over the sleeve of her woollen cardigan. Finally she glanced at Gently, who gave a little shrug and the ghost of a smile.

'You have a maid who sleeps in your wing with you, Mrs. Page?'

'Yes . . . I have.' She looked surprised.

'Her bedroom is close to yours?'

'Yes, it's on the same floor.'

'Last night after the party . . . did she help you undress?'

'No.' A rush of colour flooded the waxen cheeks. 'You must understand . . . she is indisposed. She had a heavy cold, and went to bed directly after tea. She is in bed now. She has been feverish for two nights.'

'I am sorry to hear that.'

'In fact, last night I looked in on her after I went up.'

'She would be asleep, would she?'

The colour deepened. 'You did not expect me to waken her, surely?'

'I only wished to have your word for it. At that time she was asleep, and nursing a feverish cold?'

'Yes. You have my word.'

'You would not have expected her to get up?'

'No.'

'And you would certainly not have expected her, Mrs. Page, to get up shortly after you looked in, to have dressed herself, to have gone out into the somewhat inclement state apartments?'

Mrs. Page gazed at him as though she had been thunder-struck. The colour in her cheeks ebbed and flowed and she clasped her hands tightly together in a vain effort to prevent them shaking.

'I . . . no . . . no . . . I would not.'

'And yet, apart from yourself, she is the only inhabitant of that wing, and the only other woman on that side of the house?'

'Yes . . . that is true. . . . the only woman. . . .'

Gently nodded mercifully and looked away into the fire.

'You must know, Mrs. Page, that we have a statement to the effect that a woman's voice was heard in argument in the great hall shortly after one o'clock last night, and that a moment or so later the figure of a woman was seen to emerge from the portal opposite the head of the stairs—it would be from the saloon, wouldn't it?—and go quickly through the door at the north-west corner of the gallery. Now that particular door would be the obvious choice of a person wishing to return to the north-west wing by the shortest possible route, and the north-west wing is, of course, your own, Mrs. Page. We are wondering if you would like to make a comment on this statement?'

The bracket-clock, which might have been a Tompion, impressed its leisurely ticking on the painful silence. From a great distance in the freezing dark outside came the eery barking of a dog. Each of the five men could hear Mrs. Page's quick-taken breathing.

'Naturally, you are not obliged to comment. . . .'

'Exactly,' weighed in Sir Daynes. 'Don't have to say a word, m'dear—think nothing of it.'

'Though if you do not, certain inferences——'

'Pooh, pooh!' bumbled Sir Daynes. 'No inferences—nothing of that sort. If you've nothing to say, take my advice, and don't say it—just a shot in the dark, m'dear . . . don't expect it to help us.'

The effect of this rapid little fire and counter-fire was only to make more emphatic the silence it interrupted. Mrs. Page continued to sit in statuesque wordlessness, the clock to tick, the dog, after an interval, to bark. It almost seemed as though she had lost the power of speech. But then, just as Sir Daynes was gathering his forces for another attempt, she suddenly forestalled him.

'I really don't know what comment you expect me to make.' Her voice was surprisingly steady and normal. 'If a woman was seen as you describe, then it must have been one of the servants or the weaving-staff. It could not have been my maid, and I assure you that nobody came to the north-west wing after I retired last night. Your informant was either mistaken, or else he was spying on two of the servants.'

'Just so, just so!' exclaimed Sir Daynes in relief. 'Nobody came to your wing . . . that's what we wanted to know. Lot of poppycock I don't doubt—couple of servants necking and getting up to mischief.'

Gently shook a relentless head. 'Isn't it an odd place for servants to neck? Presumably they have cosier quarters in their wing than are to be found in the saloon at one a.m.'

'I don't think it's odd at all.' Now she was facing him, the Feverell eyes stiffened with determination. 'Servants are not so predictable as you seem to suppose. They are capable of all sorts of odd freaks, especially in such a large and comparatively unoccupied house as is this.'

'Then you think it likely that two of them would be pursuing their odd freaks in that place, at that hour, after what would have been a tiring day for them, and a few minutes before a murder was committed, Mrs. Page?'

'I think it is improbable but far from impossible, Inspector.'

'I must beg to differ, Mrs. Page.'

'Then you are left with my alternative hypothesis that your informant was mistaken, Inspector. And now, if you have really nothing else to ask me, I should be pleased to go to tea.'

Gently made a gesture of neutrality and Mrs. Page, now quite in command of herself, rose and departed, the gallant baronet ushering her to the door with a volley of deprecations, excuses, and assurances. He returned very silently, however, to pace the room with an expression of mighty deliberation on his leonine face. After the third excursion he came to an abrupt standstill where Gently was leaning on the corner of the mantelpiece.

'All right!' he barked, 'all right, Chief Inspector Gently! There are two damned good theories—yours and mine. Yours says that Janice is lying, mine says that Johnson is. And out of the two of them, I'd pick mine every day of the blasted week!'

Gently shook his head sadly. 'I haven't got a theory,' he replied. 'I'm just following the ball . . . remember? I'm not responsible for the way it goes.'

CHAPTER SEVEN

TEA WAS SENT in for the policemen—after Sir Daynes had brusquely turned down an invitation to the Place table both for himself and Gently. It was no make-shift affair. Three maids with two dumb-waiters were necessary for its expedition, and the table, that important adjunct of interrogation, had to be arranged in the centre of the room and accept the dignity of a damask cloth for the occasion.

Sir Daynes was patently impatient of such a wholesale interruption. He stood by the hearth, hands clasped behind his back, pishing and pshawing as silver was laid out, the cake and the trifle installed, crackers dispensed, and a dozen seductively-laden dishes set at points of vantage. Then came two bowls of peerless fruit, a dish of mixed nuts, some boxes of dates, Chinese figs, Turkish Delight, Creme de Menthe, chocolate liqueurs, and a large case of preserved fruits. Finally, with the baronet at breaking point, a tray on which were several bottles and a box of Coronas was brought in and placed handily on a side-table.

'Confound the man!' fumed Sir Daynes balefully.

'Does he think we're giving a party, or some damn' thing?'

'You'll not be swearing on Christmas Day, Sir Daynes,' came a reproving voice from without the door.

'Eh?' exclaimed the baronet. 'What's that? Didn't see you there, Mrs. Barnes.'

'It doesna matter if you did or you didna, Sir Daynes.' The little silvery-haired housekeeper took a step into the doorway. 'It doesna become a man of your standing and principle to be making heathen oaths on such a day, and well you know it.'

'But dash it all, Mrs. Barnes——!'

'Och, there you go again.'

'I mean—bless my soul! A fine thing at a police inquiry——'

'You are not quarrelling with your vittels, Sir Daynes?'

Sir Daynes bit back an unholy expletive.

'Now just take it easy, or you'll be ruining your digestion. In forrty years there hasna been a man nor mouse in this establishment who lacked his vittels on a Christmas Day, and the good laird will make no exception now. . . .'

Mrs. Barnes departed with her minions, leaving a smirk on the face of Inspector Dyson and a broad grin on that of Gently. Sir Daynes tried to quell his rebellious subjects with a display of baronetics, but giving it up as a bad job, ordered an immediate assault on the offending tea-table. It was obeyed with alacrity. Five appreciative policemen set themselves to expunge all matters of business from their minds until justice had been done to the hospitality of

Merely Place. Crackers, alas, were pulled, and caps were worn, and Sir Daynes, forgetting the relative solemnity of the moment, laughed loud and long at a printed joke which for some reason struck none of the others as being particularly funny. He remembered himself immediately, however. From the serious way in which he lit his cigar, it was plain that he felt his hilarity to have been out of place. Christmas Day it might be, but it was a grim occurrence which had brought this odd quintet together at its festive board.

'Ring the bell and get this lot cleared away—we've still got the best part of a day's work in front of us!'

A reluctant constable, Corona in hand, went to do the baronet's bidding. Soon the table was bared and replaced in its official position, and the room, apart from lingering samples of fruit and confectionery, more in keeping with its temporary character. Inspector Dyson reoccupied the inquisitorial seat, his short-hand man took office beside him, Sir Daynes straddled the hearth, and Gently, continuing to acknowledge his role of supercargo, retired once more to the seat by the window. But before a fresh victim could be haled in there was a tap on the door, and Somerhayes entered.

'I thought I'd look in, Daynes, to make sure that you had been well looked after.'

'Eh?' queried Sir Daynes, frowning. 'Yes thank you, Henry—everything first-class. Couldn't have been better. Compliments to Mrs. Barnes, Henry.'

'If there is anything you would like sent in——'

'Nothing, man, nothing. We're damn near bursting at the seams.'

Somerhayes hesitated, as though at a loss to express himself, then he turned to Gently at the window.

'You are fully occupied here, Mr. Gently?'

'Occupied . . . ?' Gently glanced at him in mild surprise.

'I cannot help remembering that you are a guest who has been unhappily involved in this tragic affair . . . if you feel you would like to relax for a little while, my library is a very quiet and comfortable room.'

It was said with studied indifference, but both Gently and Sir Daynes caught the curious little undertone of appeal that accompanied it. Sir Daynes fired a sharp look, first at Somerhayes and then at Gently. The latter, after a moment's pause, rose slowly to his feet.

'Thank you for the offer . . . I think I might take advantage of it.'

'In that case I am glad I thought of it.' There was no mistaking the eagerness in Somerhayes' tone. 'You did not require Mr. Gently, Daynes?'

'Require him? No! Daresay we can get along on our own.'

'Then I can carry him off with a clear conscience. . . . I would not want to interrupt if he were assisting you.'

'Damn it, man!' erupted the baronet. 'Think the Northshire County Constabulary can't handle an investigation on their own?'

Somerhayes smiled humourlessly and retired with his capture.

He led the way down a long, parquet-floored corridor from the grey-panelled walls of which stared down several generations of the Feverell family, their wives and their children. He gestured to them ruefully in passing.

'Decline and fall,' he observed. 'My father hung them there, and I have not had the heart to take them down. This way, if you please.'

Gently shrugged and followed him. They had turned a corner into a small hall, and from here a door decorated with a painted armorial shield gave into the library. Somerhayes, having made way for Gently, closed the door silently behind them.

It was a large, well-appointed room with a handsomely decorated drop-ceiling and six tall windows draped with green damask curtains. The walls were completely furnished with glass-fronted mahogany bookcases, about half of them fitted with cupboards below, and a glance at the shelves showed a great catholicity in bindings and periods. Opposite the windows an ashy wood fire burned in a basket in an immense freestone hearth, the mantel of which was ornamented with shields, and above it hung framed several antique maps of the county in their original colouring and gilt. From the ceiling depended two chandeliers, but the only illumination came from a parchment-shaded pedestal lamp standing near the hearth. At an appropriate distance were arranged two wing-chairs with a table and decanter between them.

'Please sit down and make yourself comfortable, Mr. Gently. Can I pour you a glass of this port?'

Gently shook his head and selected the chair nearest the lamp.

'You will join me in a cigar, perhaps?'

'No thank you . . . I've had rather too many.'

'Like you, I find they pall if one smokes nothing else.'

Somerhayes poured himself a glass from the decanter and took it to the other chair. In spite of Gently's strategic positioning, the nobleman's handsome features were indifferently lit, and by withdrawing them slightly he could obscure them in the shadow of the chair-wing.

'You know, this is not our first meeting, Mr. Gently.'

'Hmn?' Gently was really surprised.

'No. Though I doubt whether you would be able to remember the other occasions. But I have been in court twice when you were giving evidence at the Quarter Sessions here, once at the Old Bailey, once at Lewes, and once at the Bow Street Magistrate's Court. So you see, in a manner of speaking we are old acquaintances.'

Gently nodded dubiously. 'In a manner of speaking . . .'

'More so, perhaps, than you think, Mr. Gently.'

Was there a smile playing round that thin-lipped mouth?

'As you are perhaps aware, there are few situations which reveal a man's character and personality so strongly as the occupancy of a witness-box. This is true at any level, but particularly true where such a grave matter as homicide is in question, and where the witness has a great deal of sometimes complex evidence to give, in the teeth of ruthless attacks by the defence counsel. Those are the times which try men's souls, Mr. Gently. They bring to the surface all the strengths and weaknesses, the virtues, the vices, in a phrase, the naked ego of a man. One sometimes sees one's friends as one would not wish to see them.'

'I trust I didn't expose myself too much. . . .' Gently stirred uneasily.

'On the contrary—quite on the contrary. It was by being able to observe you in these circumstances that I became so strongly impressed with your personality, Mr. Gently. I am not a man who impresses easily. By education and avocation I have learned to treat my fellow men with the greatest reserve and, I am afraid, distrust. But in your case I felt an immediate confidence, I felt that there stood a man with a deep and—may I say it?—compassionate understanding of human failings and follies. I felt this so powerfully that I made a point of being present at other times when you were likely to be called, and when I learned that you were visiting the neighbourhood, I took immediate steps to become personally acquainted. I felt, in a sense, that the hand of providence was in the circumstance.'

Somerhayes paused, watching Gently from the shadow of the wing. The glass of port in his hand glowed ruddily in the fitful firelight, and the same illumination made a livid mask of one side of his face. Gently shrugged an indifferent shoulder.

'It's a great pity somebody jogged the hand of providence.'

Somerhayes laughed softly. 'In a way, yes. But only in a way. Even this unhappy tragedy is subject to the point of view. And what makes you so certain that the hand was jogged, Mr. Gently? Could it not have moved deliberately, when a certain propitious assembly of factors was complete?'

'An assembly of factors. . . .' Gently's eyebrows rose.

'I call it that. You must consider me as being a fatalist.'

'Me . . . I'm just a realist.'

'That is your privilege, Mr. Gently.'

'I can see it in only one way. A young man who I liked has been killed . . . literally, on the threshold of life.'

Somerhayes' head dropped a little. 'I, also, was fond of Lieutenant Earle.'

'By way of corollary, there's a killer at large.'

'And killers must be stopped—you are talking to one who has heard all the arguments. Yet consider a little, Mr. Gently. The ways of providence are not our ways. A young man is killed. Another life must be given for his. Will you say outright that the event is devoid of pattern, and that a meaningless brutality has taken place and will take place? I do not believe you can be so positive. I believe there may be a point of view which, if it does not justify, will at least explain the occurrence and give it significance. We may not need to be divine to understand the workings of divinity.'

Somerhayes raised his glass and drank, and having lowered the glass, looked at it intently for a few moments as though giving Gently time to appreciate the point.

'And you think you have this . . . point of view?'

Somerhayes nodded slowly. 'To a limited extent, perhaps.'

'And you wouldn't mind explaining it to me?'

'I'm not sure that I can, Mr. Gently, though it may

be that you are the one man who could understand it. But it is very difficult, and very complex.'

A silence fell between them . . . how complete were the silences in that great house! In this room there didn't even seem to be a clock to break the cloistered stillness. Gently felt in his pocket for Dutt's pipe, and finding it unemptied, rose and tapped it out against the smouldering log.

'Suppose we start at the beginning?' he suggested. 'Just tell me how you came to start this tapestry business.'

Somerhayes repeated his soft laugh. 'You realize, then, that the tapestry workshop was the beginning?' he asked.

'It's where you gave up politics, wasn't it?'

'Yes . . . though it goes back further.'

'Well, go back as far as you want . . . I'm here to listen.'

Somerhayes nodded and set down his glass on the table.

'When I was in my teens—that would be in the thirties the world was still something of a place to live in. For me, I mean. For the prospective sixth Baron Somerhayes.'

Gently returned the nod . . . *he* remembered the thirties!

'My father continued to do things in Edwardian style, even up to the war. One was only vaguely aware that a world had changed and a world was dying, and that the standards to which one was born and bred were gravely suspect. Before I went to Oxford I never had any doubt. The social unrest that went on before my eyes did not belong to the world I inhabited. More important, perhaps, were the political events in Europe. They were certainly ominous, and more directly affecting the career of diplomacy for which, following the family tradition, I was being prepared. . . .'

Gently filled his pipe from his magnificent quarter-pound tin and settled himself in the comfortable wing-chair. Somerhayes was not watching him now. Retired into his shadow, his eyes were on the sinking fire, his low, balanced, cultured voice seeming to flow from him without effort or conscious direction. Had he ever talked like this before, this enigmatic man with his lost and wistful eyes? Had he ever before drawn in words the pattern of his bewildered life? He was doing it now, talking, talking. Like a film which had never been unwound, it was coming off its spool.

He had gone up to Oxford, certain and sure of himself. The world had been his, wealth, rank and power to come. He was one of the elect. He was one of a chosen race. Far away had been the rotten tooth of envy and the jealous anger of the mob. And there he had met—whom? A young man, working his way through college. An angry young man, an arguing young man, a young man who thrashed the pretensions of the callow nobleman with the scorpions of Marx and Engels and Lenin and Shaw. And Somerhayes had had no answer to those scathing propositions His naïve *Weltanschauung* had taken no notice of such perverse logic. His defences were scattered, his arguments flattened, his comfortable assumptions buried under an avalanche of vicious, destroying fact. And what was a thousand times worse, he was obliged to admire the person who had bowled him over. Jepson, as his name was, appeared to Somerhayes as the epitome of all he would like to be but was not. In despair he made the comparison—himself, the spiritually-bankrupt descendant of a family of social bandits; Jepson, the blazing prophet of a robbed and wrathful people. Could he fail to see that one was a dead branch, the other a new and irresistible shoot, in the tree of history?

'You will observe what a quandary I was in. I dared not follow the direction which my new convictions urged on me. I was not simply a private person. I was the future Lord Somerhayes. My niche was already waiting for me in the Foreign Office, in the Lords, in Society, and in the expectations of a father who had just lost his wife, and was himself already a sick man. How could I deal him such a blow as to declare myself, his only son, a Marxist, and he, my most affectionate parent, a social criminal?'

But something had had to come out of the shock he had received. It was impossible for him to continue entirely in support of a masquerade grown loathsome to him. It could not be Marxism, nor even Socialism; the most he dared do was to proclaim himself a Liberal. And this, unfortunately, was enough to set him at odds with his father, to whom it appeared as a betrayal of the great Tory tradition of the Feverell family.

Jepson had graduated during Somerhayes' second year, and with the removal of the irritant the young nobleman began to recover some of his lost equilibrium. To justify a step which had only been a compromise, he threw himself energetically into the cause of Liberalism, seeking to find there a creed which would strike a balance between the implacable op-

posites of competitive industry and social justice. He
learned many of the answers to Jepson's furious logic.
He discovered that the problem could not be stated
in terms of pure black and pure white. When he
emerged from the university he felt that to some
degree he had achieved a balanced view of the con-
temporary social situation, and that, holding on to it
firmly, he might proceed to his career with sufficient
confidence. He had been admitted to the Foreign Office, and in due course was attached to the Paris Embassy.

'At that time, although I did not know it, Leslie
Brass had just forsaken the Latin Quarter for the tapestry factory at Aubusson.'

'You didn't meet him in Paris?' enquired Gently,
breaking the long monologue.

'No. How should I have done? Our circles were
hermetically sealed from each other. But it has always
seemed significant to me that he and I were young
men in Paris together.'

'How do you mean . . . significant?'

Somerhayes' eyes dwelt on him wistfully. 'One of us
a young artist, just beginning to find the channels for
his creativity, the other . . . I won't insist, Mr.
Gently. And now he and I are together.'

'You wanted to be an artist too?'

'In a way, I suppose, though I understand its im-
possibility.'

'Could you explain?'

Somerhayes shrugged his elegant shoulders. 'I don't
know, but I'll go on trying.'

Eighteen months after he had gone to Paris Ger-
many had invaded Poland. Back in London he had

received quick promotion, and was engaged first in the tortuous relations that existed with the Vichy Government, and later in the endless negotiations and exchanges with Washington. Soon after the war his father had died, and Somerhayes succeeded to the title and a seat in the House of Lords. He had also been considerably impoverished by death duties, as a result of which he had been obliged to offer Merely Place to the National Trust. He now lived as a tenant in the petrified glories of the house which the second Lord had built with the money which the first Lord had ravished from the country at the time of the Bubble.

'In effect I have become a curator. . . . I am doing public penance, perhaps, for the sins of my ancestors.'

On his succession, Somerhayes had resigned from his post in the Foreign Office. His father had had a large town house in Mayfair, but this was much too big both for the tastes and the revenue of the new Lord, so he had sold it and bought a smaller one in Chelsea. There, for several years, he had lived a rather solitary life during the parliamentary terms. The political climate of his father's circle had made it uncongenial to him, and he was not a man who made new acquaintances easily. His predilection for art, however, had brought him into contact with several painters, among them Leslie Brass, who had now settled in Kensington and was making quite a stir with his pictures and tapestry. It was easy to detect Somerhayes' almost reverent admiration for the man. Perhaps nobody but the plebeian Brass with his buoyant self-confidence and cynical shrewdness could have aroused it so strongly. Here was Jepson again, but better than Jepson. Jepson had been a mere revolutionary, a stormbird, an iconoclast; Brass was a creator, an artist, a visionary. Once more, Somerhayes had found all he was not enshrined in another man. Once more, he was shaken from an apparently secure spiritual perch, and driven to put himself agonized questions.

'And then my cousin and her husband came to live in Chelsea. Previously I had seen very little of her, since her home had been in Northamptonshire.'

Janice, like himself, was now an orphan. Her father, the late Lord's youngest cousin, had been killed in an air accident in the thirties, leaving not much behind him, and Janice had passed from Girton to a library appointment in Edinburgh. There she had met her future husband, Desmond Page. Their courtship had been interrupted by the death of Janice's mother, but Desmond, in the interim, had passed his final exams, and now he had an appointment in a London hospital under the eye of a distinguished surgeon. He was thought by many people to have a great career in front of him.

Two years later he died, a victim of a post-mortem infection.

'Mrs. Page was cut up?' suggested Gently, as Somerhayes' voice faltered to a stop.

The nobleman nodded silently. His face in the firelight looked drawn and puckered.

'A very expressive phrase, Mr. Gently . . . yes, she was *terribly* cut up. She had nobody in the world to turn to. It was a godsend that I was there to help her through it.'

'She stayed in London, did she?'

'Yes, she stayed in London. She continued to live in their Chelsea flat in a state of—how shall I put it?—suspended animation. It was as though for a time she couldn't believe it had happened. She tried to continue her existence as though Desmond had just gone away, perhaps, and one day she would hear his car pull up again in the mews down below. Grief is a terrible thing, Mr. Gently.'

But the months had passed, and Janice begun to emerge from the shadow which had fallen across her path. In the meantime Somerhayes' political life had gone from bad to worse. He could not forget his early brush with Jepson. So much of what the young Marxist had flung at him seemed to be illustrated by the workings of the machine of which he was a part. He witnessed the persistent operation of self and class interests. He saw how truth could be muzzled, facts distorted, justice mocked in the name of expediency. And he made a bad name for himself by some very peculiar speeches. He was distrusted by both sides equally, and rated as being 'unsound.' The crisis came when the Silverman bill for the abolition of capital punishment was presented to the Lords. As a life-long abolitionist he had seen in this a charter for a new and better phase of civilization. He could not believe it would be rejected. There were no class interests at stake, it touched nobody's pocket. The question was entirely a humanitarian issue, to be decided on humanitarian grounds. And yet, it was rejected. More, it was rejected in a way which made Somerhayes feel it impossible for him to remain longer a member of that betraying convocation.

'One learns to forgive selfishness in politics, and dishonesty, and passion; but inhumanity one cannot forgive, or forget, or silently condone.'

He had made a bitter speech and left the House determined, he had said, never to set foot in it again while men were made of stone. The heart of politics was corruption, and he must turn his back on them. He knew what he would do. If he was not permitted to serve humanity as a law-giver, he would serve it by way of art. Himself a dying branch on a dead tree, he could yet provide the means for a genuine creator to express his vision. And so he had made his proposition to Brass, and Brass, having looked all round it to make sure that his independence wasn't threatened, had consented. Janice had also been approached and had agreed to join in the venture. The looms and equipment were purchased, six weavers assembled, and now, eighteen months later, Merely Tapestry was a name beginning to be conjured with by interior decorators.

Gently sat in silence as Somerhayes, by the change in rhythm natural to an orator, indicated that he had come to the end of his long relation. What was it this man had been trying to tell him . . . what was the implied relevance of this excursion into autobiography? There had been no further mention of Earle, none at all. Presumably, from his knowledge of subsequent events, Gently should now be in a position to elucidate the significance of what he had been told. . . .

'A winter's tale, eh, Mr. Gently?' Somerhayes was regarding him with his strange, sad little smile.

'An assembly of factors.' Gently heaved his bulky shoulders.

'You begin to see my point?'

'Perhaps . . . I begin to see something.'

'As things have turned out, how can one believe that your presence here was simply an accident?'

Gently grunted and felt round for a match. 'Mind if I put a question?'

Somerhayes nodded slowly.

'In this assembly of factors . . . would Mrs. Page be an important one?'

Somerhayes continued to nod.

'In fact, you're in love with her?'

'Yes . . . I have been for a very long time.'

'And she with you?'

'No. I do not think so. Naturally I have never mentioned it to her, and she was greatly in love with her husband.'

'Then you don't think'—Gently struck a match fiercely—'that she was interested in Earle?'

A flicker passed over the crimson-lit face. 'Of that I could not be certain. . . .'

'You saw what I saw—more, probably.'

'I saw she was amused by him.'

'More than amused.'

'It might have appeared . . .' Somerhayes broke off, raising his hand. From the far distance of the night had come a sound of singing, accompanied by what sounded like a bassoon, a trombone and a trumpet. Clearly it came to them in the book-lined room, the words if not distinct, distinguishable by virtue of their familiarity.

'While shepherds watched their flocks by night
  All seated on . . . the ground. . . .'

Somerhayes rose from his chair. 'You must excuse me, Mr. Gently. Those are the carol-singers from the village. They pay a visit to the Place every Christmas. . . . I must go and put in an appearance.'

Gently shrugged and blew out his match. Somerhayes left the room, not by the main door but by a smaller one concealed to look like an open-fronted bookcase. Outside, the carol-singers continued with their second verse.

' "Fear not," said he, for mighty dread
  Had seized their troub . . . led minds. . . .'

Gently sat up suddenly. A sound other than that of singing had struck his ear. Softly, furtively, the latch of the main door had been released . . . the door he clearly remembered Somerhayes closing when they had entered. He was across the room in a moment. Outside the hall was empty, but at the far end of it another door was just closing. He rushed to it and threw it open. It gave an icy blackness. He fumbled along the wall for a switch, but there was no switch to find, and hearing a door open further on he gave up the attempt and made for the sound. He was in the state apartments . . . obviously. Heavy, carved furniture under dust-sheets met his groping hands and sent him stumbling. It seemed an age before he got to the end of the room. The door was ajar, and once again he felt for a light switch that wasn't there. He stood quite still, listening. From very far away he could still hear the carol-singers and their brass accompaniment. Otherwise there wasn't a sound. He was alone in the dark with his breathing. Or was the breathing all his . . . was there another pair of lungs just a few feet away?

He may have heard something or it may have been pure instinct which sent him leaping and sprawling and tumbling away from the spot where he had been standing. At almost the same moment there was a violent crashing sound, and something ponderous and irresistible went trundling along the parquet floor. He fought desperately with the tangle of objects into which he had fallen. Footsteps sounded, running towards the lighted hall. Scrambling up on his feet, he chased after them towards the distant slit of light, but when he arrived there the hall was conspicuously and bafflingly tenantless.

A moment more, and Somerhayes came hastening round the corner of the corridor, alarm on his face.

'Good heavens, Mr. Gently, what on earth was that appalling noise?' he exclaimed.

'I don't exactly know.' Gently threw a keen glance at him. 'Perhaps if you can get some lights on down there, we'll be able to find out.'

Somerhayes darted to a switch-board concealed behind a sliding panel, and immediately lights blazed in the great state-room beyond the door. Gently led the way through it to the chamber where the disturbance had taken place. It was a long, comparatively narrow gallery lined with antique busts on pedestals. And the cause of the crash was not far to seek. An enormous marble bust, about three times life-size, lay gazing eyelessly at the ceiling from its resting-place on the floor.

Lying prone by the wall, its finial almost flush with the side of the doorway, was the ten-foot alabaster pedestal on which the bust had lately resided.

'Good lord!' exclaimed Somerhayes, going down on one knee by the bust. 'It's the Merely Euripides—no wonder there was a din!'

'It's not damaged, I trust?' observed Gently ironically.

'No, it's not damaged—in any case it's only a late Italian copy.'

He got to his feet and came back to the doorway. In the parquet floor was a welted bruise which might have been made by a cannon-ball.

'But think—if anyone had been standing there. They would have been killed in an instant.'

Gently nodded his mandarin nod. 'They would, wouldn't they?' he replied, poker-faced.

Through the state-room came running Mrs. Page with Brass and one of the weavers. Somewhere out on the terrace the carol-singers were giving the final chorus of their hymn.

CHAPTER EIGHT

'ODD THING, that blasted bust falling over like that,' brooded Sir Daynes as he presided over the Manor House breakfast-table the next morning. 'Can't see it has any connection with our job, though, eh, Gently?'

'Mmp?' Gently was busy with his liver and kidneys.

'Just damned odd—I mean, it might have killed someone. Pity there weren't a few confounded busts on the stairs, eh?'

It was a happy thought, and Sir Daynes pursued it. A well-toppled bust on the landing in the great hall would have satisfied the best of policemen. Busts did topple—they had had a bona fide example of it—and what would have been more likely than for the half-cut American to have embraced a pedestal on his trip across the landing, and gone to his doom, manifestly by his own hand? But alas, it was one thing with busts and quite another with truncheons. One did not embrace a truncheon, or having embraced, collect a fractured skull; neither, unfortunately, did truncheons wipe and hang themselves back on the wall after such encounters. Sir Daynes shelved the question of busts with a frown and came back to more practical matters.

'What did Henry talk about? Feller seems to have a crush on you.'

Gently shrugged as he unrinded a gammon rasher.

'Talked about himself . . . not about the murder.'

'Poor Henry,' said Lady Broke. 'He ought to talk to someone. He's always bottled it up too much, I'm sure that's half his trouble. What did he tell you, Inspector? Is there any chance of his marrying Janice?'

'Hrmp! Hrmp!' interrupted Sir Daynes hurriedly. 'Shouldn't say things like that just now, m'dear—position a little delicate, y'know—*sub judice* and that sort of thing.'

'*Sub judice?*' echoed Lady Broke. 'What in the world do you mean, Daynes? Surely you don't suppose that poor Henry is involved in this dreadful affair, do you?'

'Of course not, m'dear, of course not!' Sir Daynes turned a shade pink in his embarrassment. 'But just at the moment, m'dear—best to be cautious. Never know how far a careless word may go, and that.'

Lady Broke considered this while she sugared her coffee. 'Daynes,' she said, 'you *do* think Henry may be involved!'

Her husband grumbled and snorted and emitted two 'preposterouses!'

'You *do*,' repeated Lady Broke. 'I know by the way you're behaving, Daynes. And really, I've never heard of anything quite so ridiculous. Why, we've known Henry since he was a little boy in a sailor suit. I practically mothered him, Daynes—Tony and he used to go birds-nesting together.'

'I've already said, m'dear——!'

'Yes, I know what you've said. And I know what goes on in that silly policeman's mind of yours. But you listen to me, Daynes. I'm not often wrong in these matters. Henry is the last person in the world to offer violence to anybody he's been anti-blood-sport for years, and an abolitionist nearly as long. Doesn't character go for anything in these foolish enquiries of yours?'

Sir Daynes rumbled helplessly and made a despairing gesture to Gently. 'There's the feller who fancies Henry—I tell you, I'm trying to keep the man out of it!'

'Nonsense,' said Lady Broke firmly. 'You don't think hardly of Henry, do you, Inspector?'

Gently reached for his coffee and made unintelligible noises. . . .

'Didn't get very much from those weaver people,' muttered Sir Daynes as the Bentley again turned its bonnet towards the Place. 'Dyson put them through it, but it was the same damn' thing over and over. Got the impression they'd talked it over y'know—always tell, with that sort of thing.'

'Anything fresh on Johnson . . . ?' Gently ventured.

'Not sure I'd tell you if we had, damn your impertinence. But we haven't, and that's the truth. Only got the feller's own statement. I thought that young feller, Wheeler, was going to let something slip, but dash me if he didn't close up like a clam when we came to Johnson. Still got the servants to run through, but I don't expect much there.'

Things, however, had brightened up during Sir Daynes' absence. The conscientious Dyson, a great believer in repetition, had had a further session with the weavers, as a result of which young Wheeler had unclammed a few degrees. The strong man of the Northshire Constabulary's C.I.D. met his chief with a manner of something like excitement.

'I think I've got hold of something important, sir, something that will strengthen our case quite a bit.'

'Hah?' exclaimed Sir Daynes eagerly. 'What's that, Dyson, what's that?'

'It's young Wheeler, sir. He's admitted some information about Johnson.'

'Johnson!' cried Sir Daynes. 'Well—go on, man—come to the point!'

'It seems, sir, that Johnson has had a bit of a crush on Mrs. Page since he's been here. He's never come out in the open with it, but these weaver people have noticed it, and if you ask me, sir, they were in a bit of a collusion to keep it from us.'

'Hah!' exclaimed Sir Daynes again. 'Knew it, Dyson, knew it. So that's what they were holding back on. Go on—what did Wheeler say?'

'Well sir, Wheeler isn't what you'd call an observant type, and according to what he says he'd never added up the score until he heard one or two of them talking about it last night. Then he started remembering various little points about Johnson's behaviour when Mrs. Page was around, and decided there was something in it. This morning, when I had another go at him, he let it out.'

'Fine, Dyson, fine.' Sir Daynes hugged himself with

delight and took several paces up and down the great hall, where Dyson had intercepted him. 'But we've got to get the others to admit it too, Dyson—this feller is just the thin edge. Won't do just to have a witness who remembers because he was given a nudge—want simple, direct testimony on an important point like that. Have you been at the others?'

'Not since I've spoken to Wheeler, sir.'

'Hammer away at them, man, hammer away. We'll get what we want now one of them's loosened up. By Jove, this is a turn up! Jealousy on top of the rest! No doubt, Dyson, that Earle was making a play for Mrs. Page—hrmp!—in spite of the fact that Janice wouldn't have looked at him.'

'So I understood, sir.'

'You understood rightly, Dyson. Get your men in the Blue drawing-room, and start having these people brought in.'

'I have, sir. Everything is ready.'

'Smart feller, Dyson.' Sir Daynes clapped him on the back. 'Oh, and just one other thing. You've seen those fellers in the drive?'

'You mean the reporters, sir?'

'I do, Dyson—sitting there in their blasted cars, like a lot of pike watching for a minnow. Well, I won't have them in—make that quite clear to them. There'll be a hand-out later on, and I hope they get confounded frost-bite.'

A constable was dispatched to deliver this high decree—which was, in fact, a repetition of a lower-level directive already imposed—and Sir Daynes, after stamping around in the hall for a few minutes in case

Somerhayes should appear to greet him, turned to set off for the north-east wing. His intention was interrupted, however, by a sudden, screaming of brakes and a rattle of gravel from out on the terrace. A car door was slammed with impetuous vigour, heavy steps pounded over the gravel and up to the door. No bell was rung, no knocker was rapped; the sacred front door of Merely Place, for the first time in its two centuries, was ravished by the application of an irresistible shoulder.

'Where,' enquired a voice of thunder, 'where is the goddam boss of this crazy, tinpot, two-bit outfit?'

Sir Daynes drew himself up to his full six feet. He squared his shoulders, set his lips and thrust out his jaw. And he went to do battle with this untimely eruption of the United States Air Force.

'I'm Colonel Dwight P. Rynacker, U.S.A.F., Commanding Officer of Z Wing at Sculton Airfield—and I'm telling all and several that I've got some questions that need short, sharp answers!'

He was a heavily-built man of fifty or so with a melancholy, jowled face but tigerish, slate-grey eyes. He stood about five feet ten, and in spite of the cold, wore no great-coat over his brass-decorated two-tone uniform.

'By hokey, I've met some cases of obstruction since I came to this perishing island—I've met a few, and then some! But don't nobody think they're going to get away with the murder of a United States citizen—don't let them think it for one teeny-weeny little moment—because you want to know something?'

'I——' began Sir Daynes, seizing the opportunity.

'They *aren't*!' blazed Colonel Rynacker. 'No sir! Never! Not on your life! Not in this world! Not if the President of the United States has personally to arraign Elizabeth Two by the Grace of God and Senator McCarthy—they *aren't*!'

'Hah!' got in Sir Daynes crisply. 'Now if you'll just——'

'And no goddam lord is going to save his neck either—I'm telling you. I don't care if it's the classiest neck in this and six other peerages—if that's the neck, by hokey, it's going to be stretched, and Dwight P. Rynacker is going to stand by and see it done. Now—who are you?'

Sir Daynes extended his hand with simple dignity.

'I am Sir Daynes Broke, Chief Constable of Northshire, Colonel,' he said.

'You *are*?' Colonel Rynacker absent-mindedly seized the hand and began to pump it energetically. 'Well let me tell *you* a few things, Chief Constable—let me tell *you*! First off, what in the heck do you mean by obstructing the press in the free exercise of its prerogative in this case, hey? What do you mean by it?'

'The press?' queried Sir Daynes, also pumping. 'Who says the press have been obstructed, eh, eh?'

'I say they've been obstructed!' boomed Colonel Rynacker, pumping harder than ever. 'Haven't I just been talking to those boys out there? Haven't you just sent a cop to shut down the security on them?'

'Pooh, pooh!' countered Sir Daynes. 'They will receive all the necessary information——'

'Yeah, yeah—then why aren't they in on the case?'

'In this country, Colonel——'

'In this country you can hush it up!'

'In this country we do not permit——'

'It's a goddam lord, so you put a muzzle on the press!'

'We do not permit the publication of information which may prejudice the subsequent trial!' barked Sir Daynes, irritation getting the better part of diplomacy. 'The press are kept informed, sir. As far as we can do so without prejudice, we give them every facility to report on the progress of a case. But we do not permit the press to obstruct us in the course of our duties, neither do we permit them to publish—and, sir, I may say that they would not want to publish—anything likely to interfere with the free exercise of justice!'

'Gimme back my hand!' bawled the Colonel, dragging it away from Sir Daynes, who was performing prodigies with it. 'Great suffering catfish, do you have to dislocate a man's arm while you're laying the goddam law down? I had rheumatism in that arm ever since I set foot in this fog-happy corner of nowhere!'

Sir Daynes relinquished the afflicted member, but the light of battle ceased not to gleam in his eye. Colonel Rynacker nursed his arm fondly and made experimental movements with his fingers.

'Preposterous accusation!' snorted Sir Daynes.

'Yeah, I can see it spread over the *Herald-Tribune*,' said the Colonel.

'Doing our duty, sir, regardless of rank or nationality!'

'Doing mine too, Chief Constable, and don't try obstructing the United States Air Force.'

'Obstruction, sir!' rapped Sir Daynes, rearing up.

'You seem obsessed with the idea—who in the world is obstructing you, sir?'

Colonel Rynacker's eye wandered over the stone-cold walls of the marble hall, and returned to the baronet with the ghost of a twinkle.

'You are, you goddam old war-horse!' he replied. 'What d'you mean by keeping a rheumaticky U.S.A.F. Colonel hanging about in this sonofabitch of an ice-box—do you want to kill me off before I can get my hooks in you?'

It took a certain amount of Merely Place Scotch and a good deal of hard, factual talking to get Colonel Rynacker out of Sir Daynes' grizzled locks. The martinet of Sculton Airfield was full of dark suspicion about events at Merely, and much sold on the idea that if Lord Somerhayes was the culprit, it would need the U.S. Military Police to put him well and truly on the spot.

'Be honest, Bart! . . . just when was the last occasion that a British lord was strung up on a homicide count, huh?'

Sir Daynes wrinkled his brow, but could think of no such occasion. Gently, on being applied to, was able to suggest the execution of Laurence, Earl Ferrers, in 1760, for the taking-off of his steward, but the two centuries succeeding had been very low in distinguished gallowings.

'And what's the answer?' demanded Colonel Rynacker triumphantly. 'I ask you, is it logical that these guys knock off a lesser percentage than their neighbours? you tell me that! And if they do knock them off, how come they don't never get strung up

like you and me—what makes me think they're goddam fireproof?'

He departed at last, appeased if not satisfied, and
an anxious Sir Daynes went hot-foot to the scene of
the interrogations. Here, alas, there was small comfort
to be had. Inspector Dyson had been hammering as
directed, but all his smithwork on the weavers had
struck out little in the way of sparks. As a body, they
had gossipped about Johnson's weakness for Mrs.
Page; as individual witnesses they refused to give positive and undeniable evidence of fact.

'They're a confounded trades union—that's what it
is!' snapped the baronet, wringing his hands an-
guishedly. 'Can't they realize, between them, that
we're trying to pin a blasted murderer? Get Johnson
in here—that damn' feller has *got* to talk!'

Johnson came in, looking sullen and dangerous.
There was no doubt that by now he had realized the
role he was being cast for. He sat down without being
asked, and deliberately rolled himself a foul-smelling
cigarette. A lesser man than Sir Daynes might have
quailed under the vindictive stare the Welshman gave
him.

'Now, Johnson——' began Dyson, in a brook-no-
nonsense tone of voice.

'Well?' fired the ex-miner, the word coming like a
bullet.

'I think I should warn you, Johnson——'

'It's kind we are!' interrupted the Welshman, spew-
ing shag-smoke at his interrogator.

Inspector Dyson rose to his feet. He was no mean
figure, when it came to comparisons. He leant across
the table, his two large fists supporting him, and gave

the Welshman the benefit of a grade one Inspectorial
drilling.

'Just before we go any further——'

'Aye?' broke in Johnson.

'We'll remember where we are, and who it is we're
talking to!'

A little smile turned the corners of the Welshman's
mouth. A dreamy look stole momentarlly into his
blazing eyes. 'Ohhh!' he said, with deceptive softness.
'The Inspector wants to make something of it—yes, he
wants to *make* something of it!' And he drove a jet of
smoke straight into Dyson's face.

It happened so quickly that there was no time to
intervene. The goaded Dyson swept a fist which
should have decapitated his seated tormentor. Instead, it swept the air. Instead, something with the
jolt of a pile-driver sent him reeling back into his
chair.

'Do you *like* it!' roared the Welshman. 'Do you *like*
my little right hook, man? If you come outside a moment, I will show it to you again—though you will
have to be a bloody sight faster, if you are going to
see it coming!'

'Arrest that man!' bawled Sir Daynes. 'Gently—Potter! Grab him before he does for someone else!'

'Before I do for you, more like it!' shouted the enraged Johnson. 'Do you think I don't know, man,
what you are trying to pin on me?'

Nevertheless, he was brought to order with the
minimum of physical persuasion. That one, beautiful
punch out of nowhere seemed to have soothed the
overstrung pugnacity of his nature. Dyson was picked
up and restored to office, Sir Daynes smoothed his

ruffled plumage, and the constable, Potter, stood resting a dutiful hand on the prisoner's shoulder.

'Hrm-hrmp!' snorted the baronet. 'You've just made a confounded mistake, my man—confounded mistake. Going to commit you forthwith—assault on a Police Officer. And damn lucky you'll be if you walk out again in a hurry.'

'What is that?' demanded Johnson, the truculence rising again in his countenance. 'Are you making a charge, man—is that what you would be saying?'

'I'm expressing an opinion, blast you!' retorted Sir Daynes hastily. 'Dyson, get on with the job, and see what this feller has to say for himself.'

Dyson, chastened but ugly-looking, did as he was bid. Certain facts had come to their knowledge, he said, as a result of which they thought that Johnson might like to add to his previous statement. Johnson, perhaps, knew to what he was referring?

The Welshman sneered. 'I know as well as yourself. You have got out of Wheeler that I think Mrs. Page is a fine woman—and who, among those present, will call me a liar?'

'Our information, Johnson, goes further than that. We are given to understand that you are infatuated with Mrs. Page.'

'Infatuated, he says! There's a good copper's word for you!'

'Do you deny the truth of that?'

'Aye, unless you can find a better word for it.'

'You will be advised not to prevaricate, Johnson. Do you deny the truth of it?'

The Welshman looked at him with profound contempt. 'I have said what I have said. Find me a better word.'

'Stuck on her, man!' broke in Sir Daynes impatiently. 'Sweet on her—in love, by gad! You know what the Inspector means.'

'You have given me the word.' Johnson was silent for a moment. 'I need not tell you this, and hard would it be for you to prove it. But I am not a liar, no, and I am not a murderer either, whateffer ideas you have in your mind this moment. So I will tell you the truth, and care nothing what you make of it. I am sacredly fond of poor Mrs. Page.'

'Hah!' exclaimed Sir Daynes, moving closer in his excitement. 'Sacredly fond, eh? That's a new way of putting it.'

'New it may be, but true it is also. I would not have you think that I thought of her wrongly.'

'But you didn't like Earle hanging around, all the same, eh?'

'No, I did not.'

'Feller was a Yank—might not have been so sacred?'

'I will not conceal that I often thought otherwise.'

'And that's why you had it in for him?'

'That is one reason.'

'Best one of the lot, eh? Sort of reason that might lead to something.'

Sir Daynes eased back in triumph, leaving the examiner to Dyson. It was only by an effort that the baronet was restraining himself from rubbing his hands. Dyson, his prey restored, hastened to apply the *coup de grâce*.

'May I make a suggestion, Johnson?'

The Welshman said nothing.

'May I suggest that you now tell us the truth about what happened the night before last?'

"Read it," said Johnson briefly.

'Read it?' Dyson was thrown temporarily out of his stride.

'Read it, I said. Did you not take it down yesterday?'

'Not what you said yesterday!' yapped Dyson. 'I'm talking about the truth. And it wasn't the truth when you pitched us that yarn about going to the library for a book that night, was it? You'd got a far better reason for leaving a nice snug bed. Do you want me to tell you what it was? Shall I jog your memory about how you got Earle out on the landing?'

'I am not a *liar!*' exploded the Welshman, his anger suddenly flaring up once more.

'You're not, aren't you?' Dyson was well under way. 'But I think we're going to prove otherwise, my fine hot-tempered Welshman. Do you think the police are stupid? Do you think they can't put two and two together? They can, you know, and a good deal faster than you seem to think. Now—when did you slip Earle that message that Mrs. Page wanted to meet him in the great hall?'

'I have not slipped any message.'

'Then how did you get him out there?'

'I did not get him out there.'

'He was sleep-walking was he?'

'I told you, he was arguing with a woman——'

'You admit he was there, then?'

'I admit what I have said.'

'Yes, and you've just said that he was there—I thought you said you weren't a liar. . . ?'

Gently sighed to himself and rose quietly from his window seat. He had heard it all before . . . his whole life seemed to have been spent listening to policemen trying to make bricks without straw.

'Think I'll take a stroll . . .' he murmured to the absorbed Sir Daynes.

'Eh?' replied the baronet. 'Here, just a minute, Gently!'

He dragged himself away from the proceedings and accompanied Gently to the door.

'Well—what do you think now?' he demanded. 'Hasn't Dyson got him rocking, eh? And a blasted assault charge for a bonus—feller played right into our hands.'

Gently smiled at Sir Daynes' enthusiasm. 'I wouldn't force the pace too much, though.'

'Force the pace?' Sir Daynes sounded incredulous. 'Why, the feller will talk himself to the gallows!'

Gently shook his head unconvincedly and opened the door. Sir Daynes watched him go, an injured expression dawning on his patriarchal face. He was beginning to understand how certain Superintendents of his ken could feel when the Central Office man was treading on their sacred toes.

CHAPTER NINE

SOMEWHERE about the great house thirty or forty people were disposed, but, as always, it seemed entirely deserted. The multiplicity of rooms, their size, the thickness and solidity of the walls, all these contributed to a sensation of emptiness, remoteness and uncanny silence. Referring to his guide, Gently set off to find the south-east wing. His way took him along the entire front of the house, passing through the great hall, and though this must have been one of the principal thoroughfares he met not a soul on his journey.

The south-east wing was vaguely similar in lay-out to the north-east, and a brief reconnaisance brought him to the room corresponding to the Yellow drawing-room. He knocked and entered. The five *tapissiers* sat in a subdued group about the hearth. Closing the door behind him, he went across to the group, and stood for a moment warming his hands at the blaze.

'Not intruding, I hope ... ?'

'Naw.' It was Percy Peacock, the bald-headed little Lancastrian, who answered him.

'I should think it's warmer outside than it is in the state apartments.'

'Ah, it's a proper boom-noomber out there.'

Gently pulled out Dutt's pipe, now beginning to lose its rough edge, and filled it with leisurely fingers. They watched him silently. He could guess at the conversation he had interrupted. Three men, three women, diverse in age, character and district, the weavers were one jealous unit when it came to interference from outside. It mattered nothing that Johnson had made himself unpopular. That was purely a domestic problem. When trouble came to him, he was first and foremost a weaver—like the Musketeers of fable, they were one for all and all for one.

'Got a light, anyone?'

Percy Peacock produced a box of 'Swan.'

'I got fed up with the interrogation . . . thought I'd give you people a look. The local boys don't seem to be getting very far with the case.'

He puffed away absent-mindedly for some minutes, as though his pipe and the fire met all his requirements just then. He could feel them relaxing a little. The reference to 'local boys' had set him a little apart from the machinations of the Northshire County Constabulary. . . .

'Anyone here got a hunch?'

They didn't rise to it, but then, he hadn't expected them to.

'Me, I'm just a visitor . . . it's difficult for me to weigh things up. The local lads seem pretty sure of themselves, and perhaps they're in the best position to judge. This Johnson of yours seems to fly off the handle without much warning.'

Now there was a little stir, and Percy Peacock glanced up at him warily.

'There's nowt wrong wi' our Hugh, except he's Welsh.'

'Well, he's got a deadly right hook on him.'

'That's nobbut against him.'

'It is at the moment . . . he's just pasted the local Inspector a corker.'

'Ay?' exclaimed Peacock. 'You mean yon object wi' the teeth?'

'Inspector Dyson. He took a swing at Hugh.'

Peacock scratched his bald head and tried to conceal his pleasure at this information. One suspected that Inspector Dyson had not endeared himself with the natives. . . .

'Of course, our Hugh can be obstropulous. . . .'

'I'm afraid he was guilty of provocation.'

'At same time, Inspector ought not to have raised his hand to the man.'

'As you say, he ought not . . . he's probably of the same opinion now.'

The atmosphere had definitely warmed up. They had ceased now to watch him with the vigilance of a herd of animals drawn together against a dangerous intruder. Percy Peacock was hiding a grin, Wheeler, the young Yorkshireman, was lighting a cigarette for the pony-tailed blonde who had attracted Sir Daynes's attention. Doris, Peacock's wife, was encouraging the oval-faced dark girl called Norah to bring her chair nearer to the fire. Insensibly, Gently was merging into this difficult circle. . . .

'Coom from the Yard, dorn't you?'

Wheeler glanced at him with naïve curiosity.

'Yes . . . I'm on holiday up here. Came to do some pike fishing.'

'Joost keeping eye on things, like.'

'Between you and me they think I'm a damned nuisance.'

'Well dorn't run away with t'idea that our Hugh had hand in it.'

'Mmn?' Gently puffed indifferent smoke.

'Might be he took against Bill—dorn't say he did him in. We knaw our Hugh, and he woona have done a thing like that.'

'Well there's this business of Mrs. Page, you know . . . it gives him a fair size in motives.'

'It's something they're making too much of,' broke in the pony-tailed girl quickly. 'Half of us never noticed it, that's how much it showed. Les did, of course. He's got that sort of mind. And I won't say I was completely blind to everything going on. But Jimmy there, silly little fool——'

'Aw coom now, Anne!' interjected Wheeler, blushing.

'—he never noticed it, and never would've done if he hadn't heard one of Les's cracks. But *of course* Jimmy had to be the one to let it slip, and now they're working overtime on the stupid idea that Hugh killed Bill out of jealousy!'

'Boot ah didn't knaw——!' protested the unhappy Wheeler.

'Well you *should* have known, Jimmy, that's all I

can say, and if they hang Hugh it will have been all your fault!'

Poor Wheeler hung his head. He was obviously much taken with the piquant little blonde, and much impressed with the heinousness of his blunder. It was Peacock who half-heartedly came to the youngster's aid.

'Give oop getting at t' lad, will you, Anne? Thaws ferrety coppers'd get blood out of stawn, let alawn human being-gs.'

Gently grinned at him. 'Present company excepted . . . ?'

'Ah wouldn't like to say that till I'd seen thee gaw about it!'

Gently took another puff or two without venturing to put a question. There was no possible doubt that the weavers were behind Johnson—not merely as one of themselves, but because they were convinced of his innocence. Surely, then, they would have thought of alternatives to Johnson . . . and surely one or another of them would have observed something that might point elsewhere?

'You're positive that nobody else had a quarrel with Earle?'

'Nawbody that we knaw—you might look a little higher oop.'

'Lord Somerhayes, you mean?'

'I mean it wasn't one of us—I say nowt apart from that.'

'Someone must have broken in and done it!' exclaimed the pony-haired girl. 'There's just nobody in the house would dream of hurting Bill. *I* say the police didn't look properly when they first came yesterday. If they'd really made a job of it they'd have found where someone broke in, and then all this unpleasantness need never have happened.'

'A very tempting theory, my dear,' said Brass, who had just come in. 'If I were you I'd go and break a window, and then we'll cart the Inspector off to look at it.'

'Oh Les, I'm being *serious*!' The little blonde sounded aggrieved. 'You're *always* making fun—and there's poor Hugh in there . . . !'

Brass patted her shoulder matily. 'Cheer up—they won't hang Hugh. And descending from the sublime for a moment, what happened to that hank of purple you should have dyed for me before Christmas? I've just been hunting through the shop for it, and I've a shrewd suspicion it wasn't done.'

It was, the blonde girl protested, and she gave a minute description of where it had been left. Brass paused to light a cigarette. Around him, the weavers wore expressions of affectionate respect. To them, at all events, Brass was a giant in office, and feeling conscious of their adulation he shot one of his cynical glances at Gently.

'Want to take a gander at the workshop?'

Gently shrugged. 'Is it heated, by any chance . . . ?'

'Heated my foot!' Brass laughed aloud. 'This is art, my son, pure and unadulterated. Come and have a look, and don't be such a bloody bourgeois!'

Gently grinned and followed the artist out of the snug common-room, albeit with some regrets.

'Did you get anything out of 'em?' exclaimed Brass, as he plunged into a frigid corridor.

'Can't say I did . . . except that there was nothing to get.'

'You'd have been lucky anyway, with Hugh going through the boiler. We're a clannish lot of bastards, you know. *"Nemo me impune laccessit"* is our motto.'

'Do you think Hugh did it?'

'Me? I wouldn't be a bit surprised. When you get a bunch of queers together like our *tapissiers,* murder is liable to be the least of your problems. Why—are you joining the wagon on poor old Hugh?'

'No . . . not yet. But I was wondering if you were.'

'You can count me out, sonny. What gave you the impression?'

'It was something you said that made Wheeler wake up to the Mrs. Page angle. What you say carries weight here, and it just occurred to me that you may have had some doubts.'

'Not about Hugh biffing the young heathen, you cunning old so-and-so! He's too old and too disillusioned about women to run amok with truncheons. But hold your breath for a moment. We're approaching the sacred shrine. In the usual way we make visitors leave their shoes outside the door.'

They had come out into a building which bore all the marks of having been built as a coach-house. The walls at one side had several wide doorways, now bricked up, and the beams overhead suggested that a loft-roof had been removed. A great deal of glass had been let into the roof, in addition to long, steel-framed windows in the walls, and a double row of multiple neons flickered into brilliance as Brass brushed down the switches. There were seven looms in the shop. Six of them, placed in double rows, were flat, and had pedals, rather like so many grand pianos. The seventh stood at the far end and was of a completely different pattern, standing upright, and braced to the wall and the near-by beams. All of them were covered with dust-sheets.

'*Voilà!*' Brass struck a pose humorously reminiscent of a gentleman in an eighteenth-century engraving. 'Napoleon visited the Gobelins—why shouldn't a Chief Inspector of the Yard visit the holy place of Merely?'

Gently shrugged agreeably and allowed himself to be ushered to the first of the machines.

'This is Hugh's outfit.' Brass threw back the dust-sheet. 'That's off his own cartoon—you can see the original sitting there under the web.'

Gravely Gently examined the unfinished tapestry, part of which was taken up on a roller. It was obviously the piece on which Johnson had been working when Earle had first made his appearance—a majestic but subdued composition depicting the great Snowdon cone pressing through wispy cloud, with Crib Goch and the Llywedd Cliffs flanking it. Brass poked the warp open with a sensitive finger, and beneath it Gently saw the original water-colour drawing from which the Welshman was weaving.

'In more straightforward work we sketch the design on the warp, but Taffy is an artist and won't put up with such newfangled techniques. He interprets his cartoon like the great men of old.'

'The others work from your cartoons?'

'Yes—Hugh and I are the only artists here. And a damn' good job too, or we should never make things pay. In these hard welfare times it's absolutely essential to produce a lot and produce it quick. I learned that from Lurçat at Aubusson. I've adopted his coarse warp method, and developed a cartoon vernacular that cuts out intermediary tones and gets its effects with twenty-four standard colours . . . in addition I use a high degree of stylization and simplification in the units of design, which makes for simple weaving and also uses the coarse warp to the best advantage. As a result of these techniques we are very much a commercial proposition. We produce striking and original tapestry—modesty in a bourgeois failing—in a comparatively short time and at a comparatively low price, while the use of pure tones makes our work about as fade-proof as it comes. I don't say that the commercial possibilities weren't part of the attraction for Earle'—Brass shook his head sadly—'we've already sounded the American market, and it looks like being a big thing. My trip over there in the autumn was going to be largely a business trip.'

They moved to the next machine, which was Peacock's. A tapestry was in progress on it very different to Johnson's sombre design. This one was splendid and blazing with breath-taking primaries, it was bold and simple and executed in a sort of facile shorthand.

'See what I mean? This sort of thing takes only a week or two. That way of handling flowers and foliage cuts out all the fiddling intermediary work. . . . Peacock can weave one of those nasturtiums in an hour, and at a short distance it gives the same effect as one laboriously copied with a hundred or so tones. Not quite, of course—but then, it isn't meant to. The design calls for stylization, as you can see. . . .'

Hands in pockets, Gently followed him round. Loom after loom was unveiled, and the work examined and dwelt upon. One could not be bored with Brass. His perpetual zest conquered the marble atmosphere, the reek of dyed wool, and the overtone of tragedy that haunted the workshop. One could understand the reverence of his little company, the wistful homage of Somerhayes. Here in truth was a creator, a builder, a dynamic original of a man. His self-confidence was infectious. One felt that no obstacle could impede him. He dreamed his dreams, projected his plans, and wrestled his intent out of a reluctant world. His very name sounded a challenge in the galleries of polite and bred-out Feverells, lost and execrated Lords of Somerhayes. To what other altar could the last of a failing line take his worship, where else sacrifice the diminished booty of his race?

'And this other loom . . . I suppose that's what it is?'

Brass clapped him on the back. 'Now you're going to see the work of the maestro. I'm a damned snob, Gently—let's face facts. I learned my trade at Aubusson, but I'm a Gobelins man at heart. At Gobelins they've done high-warp weaving since the beginning of tapestry, and sheer, sniveling, miserable snobbery has driven me to fit a high-warp loom here for my own personal use.'

'It's a superior method. . . ?' hazarded Gently.

'Not on your life—just slower and more backaching. But all through the centuries the Gobelins factory was turning out class tapestry on high-warps, and a sort of legend has grown round this type of loom. So when Brass sets up, blast his feeble-mindedness, he has to have a high-warp to satisfy his ego. . . .'

Energetically the artist whipped off the dust-sheet. The high-warp loom, simple, massive, was provided for a far larger web than the horizontal machines with their treadles. And such a web was spread across it, awesome in its complexity, an irregular third of it woven in and beginning to be taken up on the lower roller. Here was obviously something different from anything they had seen before. The weaving was so infinitely fine and close, the colours so subtly graduated, that one had to look at it closely to establish that it was a shuttle and not a brush which had achieved such effects.

'Recognize it?'

Brass was quizzing Gently in his sardonic way.

'There's something vaguely familiar. . . .'

'It's Reuben's "Rape," my son, done in the best Gobelins style. I made the cartoon a year ago, and that's how far I've got, working off and on.'

'You mean that's taken you a year?'

'With my other jobs—designing, dyeing, overlooking and what have you.'

'And when will it be finished?'

'In eighteen months, perhaps . . . it makes you think, doesn't it? On an economic basis I should have to ask at least a couple of thou for it, and that's mere sweated labour.'

They stood together silently looking at it, glorious but monstrous in its witness of unbelievable effort. Only a Brass could have set his hand to such a crush-

ing burden of labour, only a man galvanized with
prodigious and unquenchable self-confidence!

'And do you think it's worth it . . . ?'

'Of course not, you bloody bourgeois.'

'At the best, it's only a copy. . . .'

'You don't know the worst, sonny. In twenty years
four hundred of the tints I'm using there will have
faded or darkened. I give that piece ten years after I
take it down.'

'Then what's the object in doing it?'

Brass shrugged his shoulders. 'Christ, a man has got
his ego. There's nobody else in this country can do a
job like that, probably nobody else in the world. How
do you think I prove I'm boss around here?'

Gently shook his head. 'It's as good a way as any
. . . I daresay Somerhayes is duly impressed.'

'Somerhayes!' Brass chuckled. 'Didn't he call you to
a session last night? I could see it coming off from the
moment he clapped eyes on you.'

'How do you mean . . . ?'

'Why, you're his natural soul-mate. Our lordship
just yearns for some Tiresias or Christ-type to pour
out his sorrows to. I'm no bloody good—he knows I'd
laugh my head off. But you, well you're born to it,
with that father-confessor look of yours. How far am
I wrong? Go on—you tell me.'

Gently put a match to his pipe, which was as cold
as the prevailing climate. 'And you fancy him?' he
said. 'You fancy him for a suspect?'

Brass was pulled up in a moment. His expression
changed completely. 'Enough!' he replied severely.
'Enough, Mr. Chief Inspector. I'm still eating his salt,

and I'm not prepared to discuss business. The most I'd say about his lordship is that he's as balmy as a coot . . . now if you'll just come through here, I'll show you how a craftsman dyes his wool.'

CHAPTER TEN

GENTLY LEFT Brass amongst his vats and turned his steps towards the north-east wing again. The omnipresent chill seemed to be eating into his bones, and he yearned to straddle before a really scorching fire. A grave of a house. Had it ever been warmed? Would the crater of Etna suffice to make habitable its dead and frozen beauty? Even its brilliant architect had admitted the futility of trying to live in it, had tucked the inhabitants away in possible but inconvenient annexes. . . .

Coming back to the great hall he hesitated, and then mounted the marble stairs and pushed his way through the portal into the saloon. Here, if Johnson was to be believed, an argument had taken place . . . but arguments, alas, rarely left visible traces. The carpet was down, certainly, and given a particular set of circumstances, some marks here near the door might have told a suggestive story. But the circumstances did not obtain. Numerous feet had passed through the door since early Christmas morning. And in real life at all events, people did not drop initialled handkerchieves at convenient spots, or otherwise make easy the lives of half-frozen policemen. . . .

He shook his head and moved to go firewards once more, but as he turned he became aware of a figure which had suddenly and silently materialized in the portal behind him. It was Mrs. Page. Her face was blanched and her eyes staring horribly. And as they stood facing each other she gave a queer little moan, and began slowly to slide down the side of the marble doorway.

'I'm all right . . . just give me a minute.'

Gently had caught her before she fell, and now she lay a dead weight in his arms, the lids fluttering convulsively over her closed eyes.

'I came to find you . . . it's stupid . . . I didn't expect to see you there.'

The breath was coming quickly, turning to vapour in the nipping air.

'You see, Henry says you're the one . . . you're the one it's going to be. . . .'

Gently made a move to carry her to a convenient chair, but she clutched his arm violently, and by a tremendous effort managed to brace her limp body. Her eyes flickered open, the pupils large and wild. Something like a ghastly smile twitched at her lips.

'I'll be all right . . . really.'

'Shall I call your maid, Mrs. Page?'

'No . . . just hang on . . . this is really too silly.'

'Can I get you something—some brandy, perhaps?'

She signalled a feeble negative. 'I've got some . . . back in my wing.'

For perhaps a minute she continued quite still, struggling to regain control of herself. Then a degree of strength seemed to surge back into her limbs, and she gently released herself from the arms which supported her.

'Help me back to the wing, will you? . . . I think I can manage to walk.'

'Don't you think you should sit down for a little?'

'No . . . help me back to my wing.'

She was inflexibly determined, so he tucked her arm under his and guided her slowly through the dreary labyrinth to the north-west wing. Here, in a small, very-feminine room, a fire was burning and a sniffling maid going round the ornaments with a feather-duster. Mrs. Page allowed herself to be seated in a chair by the fire.

'All right, Dorothy . . . you may leave the dusting now.'

'I hadn't really finished 'em, mum——'

'Never mind. That will do for this morning.'

The maid disappeared, still sniffling, and Gently located a brandy-decanter in a cabinet in the corner of the room. He poured a stiff glassful. Mrs. Page drank it eagerly.

'You must forgive me for making such an exhibition, Inspector . . . honestly, I don't do these things as a rule.'

Gently hunched an ulstered shoulder. 'You said you were looking for me . . . ?'

She nodded without meeting his eyes. 'Yes, I was. . . . I've been talking to my cousin. And then, seeing you there like that——' She gave an involuntary shudder. 'It just seemed as though you must know it all anyway—I can't help it—it seemed uncanny.'

Gently found himself a chair to his liking and reversed it so that he could lean on the back. The
brandy had brought colour back into Mrs. Page's
cheeks, but not quite the composure to her manner.

'And your cousin was saying about me. . . .'

'Oh—he says you'll be the one who'll understand
this affair . . . he doesn't think Sir Daynes has
enough imagination.'

'Do you know what he meant?'

'No . . . except that he said he'd given you a
background.'

'He's given me a background of some sort!' Gently
brooded over his chair-back. 'My imagination must be
getting rusty . . . it isn't jumping to things like it
used to. And he advised you to come clean?'

'He . . . you know about it, then?'

Gently shook his head. 'I can't help intelligent
guessing.'

'He advised me . . . I would have to have told
someone . . . he advised me to come to you.'

She had been lying, of course, when she was faced
with Johnson's statement. At the moment she had
panicked, and it had seemed the only thing to do.
The circumstance was damnable. Who would believe,
if once she admitted having been on the landing with
him, that she had had nothing to do with the subsequent event? And it was Johnson's word against
hers—or rather, the implication of Johnson's evidence
against her direct assertion: why should she not lie to
avert from herself an unwarranted suspicion?

'You must not think too hardly of me, Inspector. I
would have come out with it then and there if I

thought it would serve a useful purpose. But all it explained was why Earle was on the landing, and I knew it wasn't important, though you might have thought it was.'

Gently nodded pontifically. 'I can appreciate your feelings, of course . . . but you really shouldn't judge whether evidence is important.'

'I know . . . I know that now. I've had time to think it over. I can see that one should make any sacrifice where someone . . . someone. . . .'

She broke off with a tremor in her voice, and Gently politely looked in some other direction.

'At the same time, Inspector . . . how *can* it be important? You know I left him there—you've got Johnson's evidence. . . .'

'It could give a motive, you know.'

'A motive?' She looked across at him.

'There's Johnson, remember . . . you must know he was an admirer of yours.'

'Johnson!' She seemed genuinely surprised. 'But that's ridiculous, Inspector.'

'But you knew he was an admirer?'

'Yes—I suppose so—of a kind. But it's too far-fetched. Johnson wouldn't have killed him over me. A man would have to be frantically in love with a woman to go killing off a rival . . . and Johnson wasn't like that about me. Besides, he could have thrashed Earle with one hand.'

'Lovers are strange people, Mrs. Page.'

'I don't care. I know Hugh.'

'And you can be as certain about everyone else at Merely?'

'As certain—what do you mean, Inspector?'

'I mean there might be another admirer . . . one who *would* be in love enough to kill Earle.'

Mrs. Page remained silent for a moment, but it was not the silence of confusion.

'No,' she said firmly. 'You're on quite the wrong track, Inspector. There's nobody here except Johnson who has shown that sort of interest in me. You must remember that I have not been long a widow. My husband was a man I have not easily been able to forget. People have been very kind to me, but there have been no advances . . . nor, I assure you, would they have been encouraged.'

'Not even Lieutenant Earle's, Mrs. Page?'

She blushed. 'Not even Lieutenant Earle's, Inspector.'

Gently sighed imperceptibly and folded his arms over the chair-back. 'Perhaps we'd better start from the beginning . . . it's usually the shortest way in the long run.'

Earle being Earle, Mrs. Page had failed to take him quite seriously when he first arrived at Merely. At once he had begun to pay her extravagant attention, but since he seemed to be in the habit of spreading himself over every female he ran against, this didn't register as being particularly significant. It was just Earle's way. He was a demonstrative American. If you laughed at him about it, he laughed with you, and then went out of his way to be even more extravagant and to laugh even louder. She didn't know when it was that she first realized there was more to it. When she did, it came rather as a shock, and she didn't know quite how to handle the situation. She liked Earle very much. He had brightened up her rather

sombre existence at Merely. But she wasn't in love
with him, and she didn't want him to fall in love
with her, and now he had done so the situation was
extremely awkward.

'Under all that gay front of his he was a very sensitive person, and I was sure that he would be hurt
very deeply if I snubbed him or tried to shake him
off. He was such a boy, you know. I believe Americans mature more slowly than Englishmen. They like
to talk loudly and seem worldly and tough, but just
below the surface they are . . . well, bewildered.
Earle wanted reassuring. He couldn't quite believe in
the act he was putting on. And if I had treated him
roughly it would have shattered his confidence . . .
he didn't just love me, he needed me too.'

So she had continued on the same footing with
him, trying to hold the balance. She accepted his exaggerated behaviour as before, as though it were all a
game and a jest. For some time it was enough. She
was able to conceal from him that he was being held
at arm's length. Unfortunately, love affairs do not
stand still, and Earle, in the end, began to find the
Thou Shalt Not which was impeding his progress.

'He got very silent sometimes when we were alone
together. Naturally, I tried to avoid having a
tête-à-tête with him, but in a place like this it isn't
easy to steer clear of them. He began to talk a lot
about his people and his home in Missouri, and then
he got that *idée fixe* about us going over there on a
visit. I was the target there, I'm afraid. Les was very
largely a stalking-horse to get me to agree. I expect
poor Bill thought that once I was in Missouri my

resistance would vanish—one plate of fried chicken, and another G.I. bride would be added to the tally.'

'Did he make any passes at you?'

'Only in a playful sort of way. Honestly, he didn't know much about it, and evasive action was quite simple.'

'In public, was that?'

'No, he never did it in public. In public he kept up his Campus King act.'

'Would anyone have cause to think you took him seriously . . . that's what I'm trying to get at?'

'I'm quite sure they wouldn't. I'd say on the contrary.'

'You made it plain that it was jest?'

'Absolutely plain.'

'And you were never alone with him in a way that might have been compromising?'

She shook her head. 'He wanted to me to meet him in London—you know, Christmas shopping!—but I squashed that flatter than a pancake, both in private and public.'

'Ah well.' Gently made a humorous face. 'Go on, Mrs. Page.'

The Christmas shopping idea had been a definite invitation. He had not been explicit, but the original suggestion had been for her to spend the night in town, on the excuse that they would need a full day at the shops. When she had turned this down he still persisted that she should accompany him, and she had then invented an unanswerable rush of work-shop-business to put a final period to his importunity. He had taken this rather hardly. He had apparently built a good deal on that day in London. He had probably been under the impression that Mrs. Page's attitude was governed to a great extent by her environment, and that once she was got away from it opportunity might develop. However, he had her answer, and he had to accept it. He came back from his excursion with undiminished high spirits, and threw himself into the business of being the (slightly transatlantic) Spirit of Christmas at Merely. But there were obviously other things on his mind. His grand project, though halted, was only very temporarily postponed. After lunch he had jockeyed her into taking the walk to the folly with him, and on the way he had talked not entirely of Missouri and the old folks at home.

'He told me right out that he was in love with me, and that he wouldn't take no for an answer. Part of the time he was jesting about, talking of Christmas being the time of love and goodwill and etcetera, when people ought to let their hair down and commit a few follies. But the rest of the time he was deadly serious. He told me that he had already written to his mother telling her that he had met the girl he was going to marry, and that if I had gone to London with him he would have bought the ring then and there. Well, I did my best to keep it all in a facetious vein, but I'm afraid it was getting very difficult. I saw that soon I should have to clamp down on Bill in sheer self-defence. I think, too, that he understood the way I felt about it. On the whole, I was just a little frightened.'

'Frightened?' queried Gently, lifting an eyebrow.

'Yes—oh, I don't mean in the sense of being scared. But Bill had gone so far, you see, that he probably felt he couldn't go back, and I was trying desperately to keep the situation fluid, if you understand me.'

Gently nodded. 'You wanted to let him keep his face.'

'Exactly. And if I'd taken him seriously for a moment, it would have been all over. But I weathered that particular storm. I laughed at him all the way back to the house. When you laughed at Bill, he had to laugh back, and so we got over the walk without too much damage being done. There was just that little tension there. Once or twice, I caught him looking at me in a rather peculiar way. I felt that trouble was very definitely brewing for some occasion in the future, and I was glad there was going to be a party to give me a respite.'

During the party Bill had had to behave, and he kept his credit up manfully. There had been nothing to reproach him for. He had been his old self as ever. He had sought no tête-à-têtes, dropped no equivocal phrases, looked no odd looks. He had given a magnificent performance. It had all been saved up until everyone except Somerhayes had retired. And then, under pretext of seeing her to the door—a natural act for Bill—he had fiercely told her that he must see her alone, then, that night, as soon as he could reasonably get rid of Somerhayes.

Gently rocked forward in the chair he had been tilting. 'And your cousin—he could have heard that? He could have heard the tone in which it was spoken?'

'No.' She was quick and positive. 'That would have been quite impossible.'

'Why do you say so, Mrs. Page? You have described Earle's tone as being fierce.'

'Yes—it was. But naturally, he kept it down. Besides, my cousin was the length of the room away . . . he was pouring a drink, you remember? The drinks were on a sideboard at the far end of the room.'

'This is a silent house, Mrs. Page.'

'I know—but then, we were round the door. . . .'

'Yet you saw your cousin pouring drinks at the side board?'

'I—I mean he went to the sideboard just as Bill saw me out.'

Gently nodded inscrutably. 'Let us say he was pouring drinks. . . .'

Mrs. Page gave him a glance of quick apprehension, but there was nothing to be gleaned from a poker-faced Gently.

'Well Inspector . . . what could I do? I was afraid that if I didn't agree he would do something unforgivable—he spoke with a sort of desperation which I hadn't heard before. So I told him I would see him in the saloon in about twenty minutes, and after staring at me for a moment, he went back to join my cousin. I assure you, I wasn't very happy during those twenty minutes. I thought several times of going back on my offer. But in the state he was in, he would have been quite capable of coming here after me . . . in the saloon, at least, I would not be afraid to raise an alarm if he got out of hand.'

When she arrived in the saloon he was already there waiting for her. Apart from a gleam of light from the hall, which was lit at the lower level by a single night-lamp, the saloon was quite dark. She could not see his face. He had immediately seized her two hands and begun making violent protestations, punctuated with requests to be allowed to go back to her room with her. She had endeavoured to laugh it off, but he was in no laughing mood. She struggled to free her hands, but he embraced her and held her there by brute force. Finally, by threatening to call for assistance, she had made him release her; and after giving him to understand that he had better leave in the morning she had hurried, almost run back to her wing, and bolted the door behind her.

'And that, Inspector, is everything I have been holding back. I am willing to have it taken down and to sign a statement to that effect.'

Gently gave the ghost of a shrug. 'It's certainly a very interesting story, Mrs. Page.'

'I beg your pardon, Inspector?'

'I say it raises some interesting points—do you mind if I smoke?'

She shook her head impatiently, and he rose to empty his pipe in the hearth. Her eyes followed him as he scraped it out and filled it, and caught his for a second as the yellow flame bobbed over the pipebowl. Wariness, was it? Fear? Pleading . . . ? He remained standing by the hearth, the smoke wreathed above him.

'Yes . . . to the average police mind. You did well to ponder over this statement, Mrs. Page. For instance, the first thing that leaps to mind is that you, and not your cousin, were the last known person to see Lieutenant Earle alive . . . and that, at the most, a few minutes before he was killed.'

The blood started in the petal-like cheeks. 'I most solemnly assure you that he was alive when *I* left him, Inspector—I could hear him panting as I ran out of the door!'

'Yes, but you must look at it from our point of view, you know . . . suppose he had followed you, and you had snatched down that truncheon?'

'I—this is too absurd——!'

'And supposing Johnson, your admirer, had seen this take place. Couldn't he have thrown Earle downstairs for you, and wiped the truncheon you dropped in your flight?'

'Inspector, this is fantasy——'

'Or as an alternative theory, it was Johnson who got rid of him for you . . . if you were in danger of rape, that would be a mitigating circumstance.'

She tried to get to her feet, but her strength had failed her again. Instead she sat trembling, her big eyes fixed on him.

'Of course, I'm not saying that either of these theories are correct. They will just appeal to the police mind. At the moment the only motive they have is jealousy, and I'm sure they feel the weakness of it. Policemen are human, Mrs. Page. I'm afraid they will jump at the chance of strengthening their case along the lines I have suggested.'

'But—but it simply isn't *true*.'

'If it were, Mrs. Page, I think you would do well to admit it.'

'I tell you it *isn't*, Inspector. Oh God, why isn't the truth enough?'

'It's enough for God.' Gently hunched his shoulders. 'When you come to policemen, you're on a different footing. But you tell me it's true. For the moment I'm prepared to accept that. Now, what I want you to do is to cast your mind back over every moment of that incident in the saloon, and try to remember any little thing you haven't told me. Which way did you approach it?'

'I—I went through the Square Library and the Statue Gallery . . . and then through the west dining-room and across the landing.'

'Did you meet anybody on the way?'

'No. Nobody.'

'When you crossed the landing—think, Mrs. Page—did you see or hear anything in the least unusual?'

'No . . . I couldn't have done.'

'What sort of light is that in the hall?'

'It's a fifteen-watt bulb . . . it's down by the main door. It's just enough to illuminate the floor of the hall.'

'But there's a faint light at gallery-level?'

'Yes . . . very faint.'

'Enough to have seen anyone from the diagonals of the hall—as Johnson claims to have seen you?'

'Yes, you could just about make them out.'

'And you saw nobody?'

'I—I wasn't actually looking——'

'Or heard anything?'

'No.'

'Nor when you came out—remember, Johnson says he was there then?'

'I'm sorry.' She shook her head helplessly. 'I simply wasn't thinking about anything except what had just happened.'

Gently nodded expressionlessly. 'Very well, Mrs. Page. We'll have to leave it at that for the moment, won't we?'

She glanced at him anxiously. 'And you—you'll tell Sir Daynes?'

'Not immediately, Mrs. Page . . . I'm not an official policeman here, you understand. Perhaps we can present your . . . confession . . . to Sir Daynes less alarmingly later on. In the meantime, you have made it, which is all that matters just now.'

She offered him a tentative hand. It was shaking as he grasped it. He made a sudden face at her, which produced a half-tearful smile.

'And by the way . . . about your cousin. When did you tell him about what happened?'

'I didn't . . . he'd guessed about it.'

'Thank you, Mrs. Page,' said Gently.

CHAPTER ELEVEN

'WHERE CAN I find his lordship?'

Gently caught Thomas, the butler-valet, just as he was leaving the interrogation-room with a tray of dirty glasses. The dignified little fellow stopped politely, the tray balanced on the tips of his fingers.

'His lordship is on the roof, sir,' he replied in his smooth, careful voice.

'On the *roof*!' exclaimed Gently, staggered. 'You did say on the roof, Thomas?'

'Yes sir. He told me he expected you to enquire for him, and that is where he would be. I should add, sir, that his lordship not infrequently takes the air on the roof. It offers a considerable promenade, and the view is thought to be quite a striking one.'

'I don't doubt it for one minute, Thomas—but isn't it a bit fresh up there at this time of the year?'

'A little inclement, sir, I must admit. His lordship is very indifferent to the weather.'

'He must be!' Gently gestured to the window, through which some leafless shrubs could be seen shivering in a rising north-easter. 'Do you think I ought to have two fingers before I venture up there, Thomas?'

The little manservant permitted himself a grin. 'I would recommend three, sir.'

Gently took the advice, shaking his head. 'Crazy as a coot' had been Brass's description of the sixth Baron, and assuredly there was a semblance of reason for it. No man completely in his senses would go roof-walking on a petrifying day like this.

'You say his lordship often takes a stroll up there?' queried Gently, as the manservant waited for him to finish his drink before showing him the way up.

'Yes sir. Quite often. I believe he enjoys the sensation of solitude obtained on the roof.'

'Always done it, has he, or is this something new?'

Thomas hesitated. 'It was not so frequent, sir, before his lordship retired from politics.'

'Hmn!' Gently tossed off his Scotch. 'And he would pick to-day! Well, lead on, Macduff, and let's have a look at these historic tiles.'

A spiral stairway just off the great hall led them up to the attics above the state apartments, than which nothing could have been emptier, darker and more depressing. Through these ran a straight, narrow corridor, lit only by a few meagre roof-lights, and at the end of it a door which shielded a further spiral stair.

'This leads directly to the roof, sir,' chattered Thomas, shivering in his monkey-suit.

'Righto, Thomas . . . no need to come any further.'

'Thank you, sir. It is excessively cold. I would persuade his lordship to come down, sir, if you intend a lengthy interview.'

Gently huddled his ulster about his ears. 'I'll meet him on his own ground. Just one request, though, Thomas.'

'Yes sir?' Thomas lingered reluctantly.

'If we're not down by lunch its because we've frozen to a chimney-stack . . . you might have a rescue-party standing by to chip us off!'

The second stairway was a short one, and as he climbed it, Gently could hear the wind whistling at the door to which it led. He lifted the latch and pushed the door open. He had come up through a brick hatch projecting above the roof, backing on a sheer drop of fifty feet or so into the well of a court-yard. On either side of him the chimney-forested roofs stretched away in a gigantic rectangle. They were shallow and covered with lead, and the low coping that surrounded them offered no cover from the scourging talons of the wind. Inward, the mass of the rectangle was pierced by two wells, the one near the hatch oblong, its fellow, some distance off, a square. As far as Gently could see, he had the entire, bliz-zard-swept desert to himself. There was not a sign of Somerhayes.

Squinting his watering eyes, he set off stubbornly to make the round of the roofs. The wind, once he left the shelter of the hatch, pierced through his thick ul-ster like knives. A mad place to be . . . a danger-ous place! If you lost your balance, you could be blown over the coping in a moment. And how did the man expect Gently to find him up here, amongst the chimney-stacks, hatches, sky-lights and whalebacks of lead? Or had he expected to be found . . . was this Somerhayes' way of going to earth? Gently crouched by a stack for a moment. It could be that Somerhayes had cleverly got rid of him for an hour.

A fine fool he would be, clinging up here to these chimneys and copings, while Somerhayes, down below. . . .

But then, what could the fellow be up to?

He was half-way round before he spotted his quarry. By that time he had begun to feel that he would never thaw out again. His best trilby had blown away, his fingers were dead in their thick, wool-lined gloves, and his whole body felt shrunken and aching with cold. Then, as he rounded the coping at the corner of the square well, he saw the maddest thing of the whole mad interlude. At this point he had come to the back of the great triangular cornice which surmounted the columns of the portico at the front of the house. From this cornice was reared a flag-staff, and clinging to the flag-staff, his foot on the apex of the cornice, his body exposed to the full range of the blast, was Somerhayes. He did not turn as Gently rounded the corner. He was facing outwards, towards the wind, towards the distant, ice-flecked sea. And he was wearing nothing but the loungesuit he wore about the house. He had not even gloves on his blue, clutching fingers.

Incredulously, Gently plodded up a grey roof-back and down to the back of the cornice. The apex where Somerhayes was standing was a good twelve feet above the roof.

'Hey!' he shouted up. 'Come down before you freeze solid!'

Somerhayes glanced down over his shoulder. 'No . . . you come up, Mr. Gently!' he called back.

It was a palpable challenge, and Gently looked about him for some way to meet it. There was no ladder up the back of the cornice, but at some period a series of rough hand and foot-holds had been chiselled into the stone, and these, though badly worn, appeared to be the means by which Somerhayes had reached his dizzy peak. Slowly, obstinately, Gently began to climb.

'Use the flag-staff as a handrail . . . you'll get stuck if you don't.'

Gently grunted and felt across for it. Near the apex, the chiselled hollows were nearly worn away. By a final effort he got his arm round the staff where it cleared the apex, and by hugging it tight could just peer over into the airy gulf below.

'What do you think of the view, Mr. Gently . . . ?'

'I can't think of views when I'm being flayed to death!'

'Look . . . the sea! And the Wind of God coming off it!'—Somerhayes raised his arm and pointed outward.

Gently blinked the water out of his eyes and looked. Directly below was the terrace with the cars, Repton's artful drive snaking beautifully away from it into the gloomy grove of holm-oak. To the left extended the park and the lake, hemmed in with forbidding reefs of chestnut and oak, a driveway at the extremity stretching to the pale cupola of the folly elevated on its gentle knoll. And beyond this, over the regiments of trees, behind a strip of rough salt marsh and a white-fringed ribbon of beach, lay the iron-grey, iron-cold sea, its horizon scarcely to be distinguished from the iron-grey, iron-cold sky.

'That way came the Northmen!' exclaimed Somerhayes in a strange, ringing tone. 'On a day like this, on a wind like this, in ships without decks they sailed that sea, Mr. Gently. A thousand years ago one saw their dragon sails, and a few last descendants of those ships still sail the Northshire rivers. Go into any fishing village along this coast, and look, and look, and you will see the Northmen . . . we Feverells come of Norman stock, but whence came the Normans to set their standard in France?'

Gently screwed up his eyes and tried to get some cover behind the weather-roughened coping.

'We must have degenerated a good deal since those days. . . .'

'But have we, Mr. Gently, have we?' The crazy fellow was ripping open the front of his shirt. 'Look . . . this wind is no stranger to me. You shrink from it down there, but I can receive it with a bare bosom, steel to steel, element to element—and all I feel is its fire, scorching me as it scorched the conquerors who came here long ago. It is the world that has degenerated, we are still the men we once were.'

'Come down,' urged Gently. 'Let's talk about it in comfort.'

Somerhayes laughed, the sound of it whipping away on the lashing wind. 'Look below!' he cried. 'Do you see those steps down there, immediately below, near where that constable is stamping his feet?'

Gently poked his head over.

'There's an answer, Mr. Gently—I could have it in just two seconds.'

'What answer is that . . . ?'

'The answer to everything that troubles a mortal soul. See—it's in my hand'—he let himself swing out over the void—'five frozen fingers are all that hold the veil between myself and the perfect truth. Shall I accept it, Mr. Gently? In your present knowledge, do you advise me to accept it? Or are there still some things which only I can tell you?'

Like a reversed weathercock he hung there, smiling down at the crouched Central Office man. With a sense of shock Gently realized that the nobleman meant what he was saying. In two seconds, he could be a lifeless heap on the steps beneath. A mis-move, a wrong word. . . .

'Come down,' he repeated. 'I want to talk to you.'

'But we can talk up here . . . surely this is the ideal situation?'

'It may be for you . . . me, I'm just a bloody bourgeois. I'm going down—I'll see you later on.'

'Wait!' exclaimed Somerhayes, swinging in again.

'Sorry, I've had enough of it—see you when you get down.'

Deliberately, without looking back, he began feeling for the worn toe-holds. He could hear nothing except the moaning of the wind and the flap of the halyard against the flag-staff. Regaining the roof, he clambered over the shallow pent behind the cornice, and taking cover in the lee of the nearest stair-hatch, began to fumble with Dutt's pipe. The seconds stole by. Resolutely he packed the tobacco, his fingers stiffened like claws. He was just scrabbling in his pocket for a match when there was a footfall on the lead beside him, and Somerhayes was standing there, something like reproach in his grey eye.

'Are you the man I took you for?'

Gently tried to keep the relief out of his brief shrug.

'I felt sure I could depend on you. . . .'

'Cup your hands round this match, will you . . . it's like trying to get a light in a wind tunnel.'

Somerhayes complied with a touch of disdain. His small, fine hands looked ugly from the savage exposure they had undergone. Gently got his pipe going after three attempts. For some reason, he was being particularly clumsy about it.

'The winters you get in this godforsaken county!'

'Our summers are correspondingly fine, Mr. Gently.'

'They've got a lot to make up for . . . do people die young?'

'On the contrary, this county is celebrated for longevity.'

Finally, the pipe was lit, and Gently, setting his back against the hatch-door, puffed it till the warming bowl softened the initial harshness of flavour. Somerhayes stood by him, ignoring the friendly shelter of the hatch.

'You wanted to talk to me, Mr. Gently?'

'Mmn—just as you expected.'

'Naturally, after my cousin had spoken to you——'

'It's up to you to clarify her somewhat onerous position.'

Somerhayes glanced at him with sarcasm. 'You realized, then, that I should be able to?'

'Otherwise, you wouldn't have known enough to have advised her to make a clean breast, would you?'

Somerhayes nodded, looking away. 'Perhaps I've mistaken you after all, Mr. Gently. . . .'

The wind whipped over the hatch-top, scuffing the smoke from Gently's pipe. He moved up a little to make room for Somerhayes, and now the nobleman accepted the threadbare protection of the tiny structure.

'You were in the hall that night, weren't you?'

'Yes. I was sure you must have guessed it.'

'Would you like to say why you didn't mention it?'

'You may think, if you like, that it was because I didn't know how much Janice would admit to.'

'Suppose I don't choose to think that?'

Somerhayes' queer little smile was back. 'You are the detective, Mr. Gently, what you think must be entirely governed by your discoveries.'

Gently puffed sombrely for a few moments, his hands dug hopefully into the ulster's pockets. 'All right,' he said. 'I'll buy it. Tell me just what you want to tell me. But before we go any further, can't we get off this murdering roof?'

Somerhayes shook his head and edged away a little.

'We'll stay here, if you don't mind . . . it is a place where I have always made decisions.'

Gently grunted and tried to get his back yet further into the comfortless door.

'In the first place I knew of Earle's assignation—that must certainly have occurred to you. I was very anxious about his pursuit of my cousin, and I took steps to overhear what passed when he went to the door with her that night. The rest is quite simple. I merely took my stand at the corner of the gallery, opposite to where Johnson emerged. I was witness to the meeting. I can vouch, like Johnson, that my cousin left Earle in the way she will have described to you. I can also vouch that Johnson retired a few moments after my cousin left. Oddly enough, Mr. Gently, I suspected that you would have guessed these trifling points without any prompting.'

'They may have run through my mind.' Gently grimaced behind his pipe. 'And after Johnson retired . . . when you and Earle were left in the hall?'

'What else can I say? The interlude was over, and like Johnson, I went back to bed.'

'Leaving Earle alone?'

'Leaving Earle alone.'

'And the hall, of course, quite empty?'

'To the best of my observation, *quite* empty.'

Gently shook his head gravely. 'Well . . . that certainly seems to clear Johnson, doesn't it?' he said.

Somerhayes said nothing, but gave the Central Office man a rueful, almost reproachful look. His shirt-front was still open, his customary neat bow-tie dragged apart and hanging loose at each side. How could he stand it, that crushing, warping cold . . . how could he remain there, apparently so alert, when his face was grey, his neck and bosom bloodless, his neat hands swollen and all the colours of the rainbow? He had to be crazed, this fey question-mark of a man!

'Just *what* was your attitude toward Earle?'—Gently could almost hear the perplexity of his own voice.

'Why, surely I was jealous . . . you will not have forgotten that I am in love with my cousin?'

'It doesn't fit in. Jealousy won't sit square on your record.'

'I assure you that I *was* jealous, Mr. Gently——'

'I know, I know! But it wasn't the right sort of jealousy . . . couldn't you have had it in for Earle because he was an American or something?'

Somerhayes looked gratified. 'You are restoring my faith, Mr. Gently. Yes, you are quite right. His being American had a great deal to do with it. It was nothing against him *per se,* you understand. I have the greatest admiration both for America and the Americans—they are magnificently young, intoxicatingly virile. Purely at a surface level, one would say that nothing could be more fitting than the mating of fresh American blood with a scion of English aristocracy. But that is leaving out the personal element, and I am afraid that in this instance it cannot be lightly dismissed. I know my cousin, Mr. Gently. She is a Feverell, with all the family strengths and weaknesses. It is, unfortunately, a Feverell characteristic to be swept off one's feet, and Janice, in spite of her constancy to her husband's memory, was being swept off her feet by Earle.'

'Wouldn't that be her business?' interrupted Gently.

'Impersonally again—yes, it would. But how can one see with equanimity a beloved person rushing into unhappiness?'

'How do you know it would have been unhappiness?'

'Because, I repeat, Mr. Gently—I know my cousin. In many ways she is spiritually delicate and easy to injure. It would have been the height of folly for her to have married Earle and consented to live with him in America—as he would, quite properly, have required her to do. She is completely unfit for any such transplantation. She is a creature of her environment, and if her roots were cut she would wither away. Yet her character is such that Earle might easily have hurried her into that error, and my anxiety at what was transpiring was correspondingly intense. She is the only tie of blood I have in the world, Mr. Gently, and I feel for her as a kinsman as well as loving her as a woman.'

'Hmn.' Gently exhaled a long mouthful of smoke. 'I like that better, but it still won't focus any too sharply.'

Somerhayes flashed him a quick look. 'Have you no daughter or kinswoman dear to you?'

'No.' Gently shook his head. 'Like you, I am rather short on the ties of blood. . . .'

'Ah. I felt we had much in common. But you will still appreciate the powerful emotions involved.'

'Oh yes, to a certain extent. . . .'

'To an overwhelming extent, rest assured.'

'Very well, if you say so. Overwhelming—but not, perhaps, exclusive?'

Somerhayes pressed his thin lips together and stared out over the heavy-grey expanse of the roofs. Gently noticed the contraction of his multi-coloured hands till white spots appeared over the knuckles.

'Then I will go a little further with you,' he said slowly. 'I want you to be quite satisfied, Mr. Gently—I want your focus, as you call it, to be as sharp as you can possibly desire. There is another element that enters into this. My cousin, as perhaps you do not know, is an indispensible factor in the success of the tapestry workshop. I myself am no more than an organizer, and an indifferent one at that. Mr. Brass is a great creative artist, and cannot be expected to expend his

unique powers in matters of business, even supposing
he has the ability, which he has not. The workshop,
in effect, is entirely dependent on my cousin's shrewd
head for its business management, and my conviction
is that it would quickly come to grief if it lacked this
able hand at its helm. You are already aware of the
importance to me of this venture. I could never
willingly allow the work of Mr. Brass to be interrupted or jeopardized. You will see then, that I had here
a strong additional reason to view with concern Lieutenant Earle's overtures to my cousin. Have I now as-
sisted you, Mr. Gently, to get your picture into a
definitive focus . . . ?'

He stopped to look at the huddled figure of his
companion. There was a far-away expression in the
Central Office man's eyes, and he seemed to be listening to something not comprised by the blustering
wind and Somerhayes' smooth, level voice. Suddenly
he whirled round, grabbed the handle of the hatch-
door and tried to thrust it open, and, finding it
bolted, launched his bulky shoulder at the obstacle
with a resounding crash.

'Mr. Gently——' exclaimed Somerhayes.

'Quick!' bawled Gently, grabbing his arm. 'Which
is the way we came up?'

'The way . . . ? It's that hatch by the long court.
But what in the world is the matter?'

'We've been eavesdropped—for the second time—
that's what's the matter. And I'm getting remarkably
curious to know who is taking such a profound interest in our conversations.'

Lugging the protesting Somerhayes after him, he
scrambled off in the direction of the long court. It

was a slender chance, and such as it was it was being jeopardized by Somerhayes' apparent inability to go straight to the hatch with the unbolted door. By the time they were down in the attics Gently realized with chagrin that the listener must have had sufficient interval to make good his retreat. The eternal silence of the great house was all that there was left to hear. . . .

'Mr. Gently, I feel certain that you were mistaken,' panted Somerhayes, catching up with the detective as he whisked along the narrow corridor. 'I assure you I heard nothing . . . it is straining probability to suppose that anyone should be accidentally in the attics.'

Gently slackened his flying stride till the nobleman was abreast of him. 'You didn't hear it—and I shouldn't have done, eh?'

'I fail to understand you——'

'That's something else we have in common.'

'Your imagination, Mr. Gently——'

'Is something that doesn't topple busts!'

Savagely he threw open doors along the corridors, revealing nothing but dark, empty and cobwebbed rooms. On the other hand, the door at the top of the stairway to the main floor swung mockingly ajar. . . .

Somerhayes, like a marble-eyed spectre, stood watching him in his fruitless activity.

CHAPTER TWELVE

THE INTERROGATION-ROOM in the north-east wing was empty; Sir Daynes and Inspector Dyson, Gently was told, had jointly carried off the offending Welshman to durance vile.

'Did they get anything fresh from him?' enquired Gently perfunctorily.

'Oh yes, sir,' replied his constable informant. 'He admitted that he was in the wartime Special—knew all about the handling of truncheons, he did. The Chief Constable wants to give him one to see how he would go about it, only our Inspector don't much like it, so the C.C. scrubs round it.'

'Just as well for Inspector Dyson.' Gently permitted himself a grin. 'And that was all—after two hours interrogation?'

'Well, they trips him up a bit, sir—you know how it is. And there was something about him killing a sheep-dog with a bottle when he was a nipper—dog jumps out at him, and he fetches it a clout with a pop-bottle.'

Gently clicked his tongue. 'I wouldn't have said that was habit-forming. There was no charge made, was there, other than for assault and battery?'

'No sir. Not yet. But between you and me, sir, it's working up to it.'

Gently stood brooding in the empty room with its settling fire and suggestive disposition of chairs and table. With the light switched off, it looked doubly depressing. The corners were full of gloom which the north-facing window failed to dispel. What effect did it have on the character of its inhabitant, this mighty museum of perished vanity, how did one, tethered here, adjust oneself to the rushing current of the world outside? 'A hymn of the eighteenth sounding sweet in the ears of all centuries succeeding'—that was the quotation the author of the guide-book had dug up out of somewhere. But it was a hymn with forgotten music, a hymn of which only the antique words remained. And, in the meantime, a godless generation had camped at the gates of antiquity, unleashing its Jepsons and Brasses to sound chaos through the halls of pomp and circumstance. Would not the last lonely chorister be baffled by the universal shout? Would he not waver and lose the thread, and lose himself, and lose his balance . . . ?

Unconsciously Gently shook his head at the dying fire. But you couldn't put history in the witness-box, either for the defence or the prosecution! A number of the cruder facts and a presumption of responsibility . . . that was the substance of justice in a court of law. But what were the facts of this case, and how far dare one to presume? What blindness and double-blindness awaited the trier-on of justice?

'You are not returning to the Manor House for lunch, sir?'

Thomas had stolen noiselessly in with a fresh chute of coal.

'I'd forgotten about it, Thomas . . . any prospect of a bite here?'

'We keep an excellent table, sir, in the south-east wing. In the usual way his lordship patronizes it, but to-day he is being served privately with his cousin.'

'Thanks for the tip, Thomas . . . his lordship and I have temporarily exhausted our small-talk.'

Without much appetite, Gently made the diagonal journey through the forsaken building, and by trial and error discovered the south-east dining-room. He was apparently late, since Percy Peacock and his wife, with Norah, the dark girl, were just leaving as he entered, and Brass was the solitary remaining occupant. The artist sat gloomily cracking nuts and drinking port. He made a weary gesture as Gently took a seat opposite him.

'God, what a bloody Christmas! It's giving me the willies. I wish I was in Kensington, and a thousand miles away!'

Gently made a face and poured himself an aperitif from a bottle which stood on the table. A face looked through the service-door, and a moment later a plate of Julienne soup was placed before him.

'Last year I made an excuse to get out of this dump—there was only Anne and Norah here then. This year there was more of a crowd, so I was brain-sick enough to give it a whirl. Never again, Chief Inspector Gently, never again in this damned round of existence!'

Brass cracked a nut so viciously that a fragment flew half across the room.

'Of course, the circumstances are exceptional. . . .'

'I wonder,' retorted Brass. 'Yes, I really and truly wonder! You say it's exceptional, because we've got an unexplained corpse on our hands. Well *I* think his lordship would make like he had an unexplained corpse on any blasted Christmas, and in that strong belief I'm going to Kensington next year.'

He finished his port, and poured another. His fiery beard stuck out discontentedly from a stubborn chin. This was Brass having the blues, his aspect seemed to say, and woe-betide the mere mortal who came between the man and his grouch.

'You've seen his lordship?' hazarded Gently.

'Yes, I've seen the damned fellow. Came moaning into the workshop, looking as though he'd seen the ghosts of his benighted ancestors. I tell you, the man's up the pole. It's inbreeding, or some bloody thing. Once I used to be charitable and think he was just a harmless eccentric, but the more I see of his lordship, the more I'm convinced that he's crackers—and so was I, when he talked me into this infernal set-up!'

Another nut distributed its shell impartially about the south-east dining-room.

'Do you know what he had the crust to ask me?'

'No?' Gently rested his spoon.

'He asked me if I'd toppled that bust over last night—serious you know, just like a blasted judge! I mean, what do you make of a man who goes round asking things like that? If I wanted to have a spree I wouldn't stop short at one bloody bust.'

There was a fresh-air nature about Brass which, in spite of his ill-humour, was a welcome relief in that house of shadows. Here, at least, was a boisterous and aggressive sanity, a mind determined to stand square on its shameless egoism. If you bounced a question on Brass, it would come back clean without a wherefore. . . .

'Seriously, though . . . do you think his lordship is quite himself?'

'Seriously, my son.' Brass screwed his large features up over a refractory Brazil. 'You know what I've said—and I'm not going back on it. But I've been thinking around, as I pottered over my dye-vats, and there's one thing that struck me which I think ought to go on the record. Somerhayes never told you about his will, I suppose?'

'His will?' Gently sat up.

'Yes—I can see he didn't get round to it. And that convinces a suspicious mind like mine that there might be a reason for it. Wait a minute, old man, till they've brought in your pheasant.'

The serving-maid appeared with the dish Brass predicted, and Gently contained himself in some impatience while she performed her various ministrations. Brass watched her with unconcealed interest. She was quite a pretty serving-maid. . . .

'As you were saying before we were interrupted . . . ?'

Brass nodded and tossed off his second glass of port.

'It's not so much the will—I imagine that's pretty straightforward. It's what hangs to it that makes the thing suggestive. You've got a fair inkling by now, have you, of where the sixth Baron and myself stand with each other?'

'He appears to admire you very highly.'

'Admires me—huh!' Brass gave an expressive snatch of his head. 'Gently, my son, that cock-eyed page of

Debrett worships the bloody ground I walk on—like a
damned heathen—like a miserable wog! He's got a fix
about artists. They do the one thing no Feverell has
ever been able to do—make something. And so here I
am, the tin god of the last of the Feverells, the sacred
calf cherished and worshipped in the high places of
Merely—with Somerhayes, of course, my self-ap-
pointed priest. Do you ask me now how far round the
fellow's gone?'

'He's got a complex character. . . .'

'Complex is hardly the word, child. If you'd lived
beside him for eighteen months . . . but hell-
an'-all, we won't go into that! Just get the picture of
Brass the God and Somerhayes the Priest, that's all
you really need to understand. Now Brass Divine all
gods excelling has got one bad flaw in his make-up.
He's a little too easy about the come-and-go of cash.
Priest Somerhayes isn't so hot in that direction himself, but by the grace of inferior gods he's got a cousin
who is—and there, my maestro, the plot begins to thick-
en. Our High Priest can't content himself with his
cousin being a mere lay-sister. Her holy duty is too
plain before her. She must take the veil, she must
espouse the Church, and by way of endowing the
sacred institution, she is to bring with her all the tin,
shekels, tenements and messuages yet possessed by the
house of Feverell—which is the substance and contents of the will I mentioned to you. Think that one
over, sonny, and see where it gets you.'

Gently gazed at his untouched pheasant as though
it were something rare and miraculous in the field of
ornithology.

'You mean she's the heiress to the estate, contingent on her marrying you?'

'Not contingent, old fellow—at least, not as far as I know. She gets it anyway. It's the bribe to make me sit up and take notice.'

'And Mrs. Page—what are her views?'

'Hell! It's not as crude as that. Janice hasn't been told—it's up to Leslie to make the running.'

Gently nodded to the pheasant. 'And of course, you haven't made any. . . .'

'Don't be so blasted cunning!' retorted Brass, grinning at him. 'Do you think I'm made of stone, to sit behaving with a trollop like that in the offing? I made a pass at her for her own sake, long before I got the wink from Somerhayes. But as I told Sir Daynes, she's man-proof, and it'll be a year or two yet before there's anything doing there.'

'Aren't you forgetting Earle?'

'No, I'm not forgetting Earle. That kid was certainly storming the ramparts, but you can take it from me he wasn't getting anywhere, and never would have done.'

Gently at last made a motion with his knife and fork, but he seemed to be eating without much consciousness of the act. Brass sat watching him with an air of devilment. He cracked a nut to give the Central Office man time to take in the significance of what he had heard.

'You were sure about Earle . . . but his lordship wasn't. Is that what occurred to you when you were thinking it over?'

Brass shrugged massively. 'Without putting too fine a point on it, as someone said.'

'In fact he might have taken Earle seriously?'

'He might. I don't say he did. But it seemed an idea worth toying with.'

'Mr. Brass.' Gently looked the artist in the eye. 'Either you think his lordship capable of letting his obsession get the better of him or you don't . . . which is it going to be?'

Brass laughed gleefully and levered his great body away from the table.

'This is where I leave you!' he said, tossing the nut-crackers on the table. 'Enjoy your pheasant, try some apple foam—and don't be afraid of that bottle of port. God Brass is going to the workshop. You'll find him there if you want to talk weaving.'

And he strode out of the dining-room, still laughing loudly to himself. But there wasn't any smile on Gently's wooden countenance.

Sir Daynes returned, looking, if not cheery, as though he felt he had coped ably with the iniquity of things. Gently met him in the hall, flanked by Dyson and a constable, and the good baronet expressed his apology for having failed to take Gently back to lunch.

'Said you'd gone up on the roof—wouldn't be having a game would they?'

Gently grinned faintly. 'No—I was up there all right.'

'Damned odd place to be, but I suppose you know your own business best. Anyway, we popped Johnson in the cooler, and he'll be remanded to-morrow. Just going to run over the servants to see if we can pick up anything fresh.'

'Naturally, you won't have charged him . . . ?'

'Not yet, man. Probably will do this evening.'

'Before you do, there's a couple of small matters worth considering.'

'Eh?' barked Sir Daynes, apprehension suddenly gripping him.

Gently hunched himself owlishly in the depths of his ulster. 'Firstly, Mrs. Page has made a statement which supports Johnson's account of his movements . . . secondly, his lordship has made one that practically exonerates Johnson.'

Sir Daynes' blue eyes opened wider and wider, and by way of support, Dyson's jumped open too.

'You said . . . *what*?' gaped the baronet in desperate incredulity.

Gently repeated his thunderbolt without any enthusiasm.

'But good God, man—we've got Johnson—got a case—this is preposterous! What do these people think they're doing, making irresponsible statements?'

Gently shrugged from his depths. 'There's still a loop-hole . . . but it's a small one. On the whole, I think we'd better discuss the matter before we go any further.'

With a lengthened face Sir Daynes led the party back to the milder atmosphere of the interrogation-room, and the face was still longer when he had heard what Gently had to tell him.

'Good heavens!' he kept interjecting. 'Good heavens! It's unbelievable! Can't call you a liar—good heavens, what a business!'

At the end of the relation he stood rigidly with his face towards the fire. His hands, clasped behind his

back, were the only barometer of his bewildered an-
guish. A long minute passed before he turned. Then
he shot a fierce, bitter look at Dyson.

'Well!' he rapped. 'Go on—you're in charge of this
blasted case.'

Dyson wilted a little and sucked his lip under his
teeth. 'Well sir, it seems to me   '

'Go on, blast you—what are you stopping for?'

'It seems to me sir . . . on the present evidence
. . . that there's a strong case against his lordship.'

Sir Daynes took a deep breath and bit his lips until
he must have hurt himself. The age showed in his
rough-hewn features more cruelly than Gently had
ever seen it. And slowly, he bowed his head.

'Yes,' he muttered through his teeth. 'Yes, Dyson—
quite right, Dyson! There's a case against him—a
strong case—a case a blundering old fool like me
ought to have seen all along! Been pointers enough,
Christ knows. Been men around me who could see it
as clean as a pikestaff. Only I'm an obstinate old fool.
I didn't want to see it, and I wouldn't. I knew Somerhayes' father . . . thought I knew Somerhayes.
Time, high time, for an old dotard to retire!'

'Johnson might have come back . . .' murmured
Gently apologetically, but the baronet shook his head
peremptorily and put a hand on the Central Office
man's shoulder.

'No good flogging that horse anymore . . . I can
see what I can see! We're going to hang a Feverell,
Gently, and no Johnson will save his skin. Mad, he
was, mad, and perhaps he'll get away with it. But into
the dock he's going, like the most beggarly killer be-

fore him. It doesn't need a United States Colonel to show me the way of duty.'

Gently fumbled around in his pockets. Somewhere there should be a forgotten peppermint cream!—An abashed Dyson, shaken by his chief's distress, made officious arrangements of the gear on the table.

'Get Mrs. Page in, Dyson.'

The baronet came out of his momentary stupor.

'We'll have to have her statement first—needn't go into details. Don't suppose the feller'll run away until we're ready for him.'

A constable made a move towards the door, but Gently stopped him with a gesture. 'If you don't mind . . . I'd rather you didn't call Mrs. Page for the moment.'

'What?' demanded the baronet. 'Why? Why not?'

'It's a difficult question . . . all this case is a bit involved. There are some psychological oddities about it that don't quite square, not to mention some of the hard, irreducible facts. . . .'

Sir Daynes didn't jump down his throat, as he would have done of yore. He was relearning his respect for the apparently vague and unofficial ways of Gently. Also, there might be some excuse for not immediately pursuing that thorny path of duty. . . .

'Well?' he prompted, with moderated severity.

'I'm not sure . . . I'm not happy about it. I'd like to talk to Mrs. Page myself before you have her in here. And Somerhayes too. . . . I can't quite pin that fellow down. We've had two bouts already, and each time he's slipped through my fingers. I've got the impression that it's going to be the best out of three.'

'You mean you think he'll confess?'

'I don't know, and that's the truth.'

'Then what are you after?'

'I'm not sure of that either. . . .'

'Damn you, Gently!' exploded Sir Daynes, with a flash of his old fire. 'Why do you want to hang it out man—why not put us out of our misery?'

Gently shrugged into his ulster and brought out his last, fluff-engrained peppermint cream.

'It's a personal matter,' he said. 'It has been all along.'

CHAPTER THIRTEEN

DOROTHY, Mrs. Page's snuffling personal maid, re-admitted Gently into the dainty little north-west drawing-room. Her mistress was dressing, she told him, she would inform her that the Inspector wanted to see her. Left alone, Gently prowled about the room in the habitual way of detectives the world over. He wasn't looking for anything . . . but anything that might be looked for he wanted to see. In the present instance there was nothing, except indications of the character of the occupant. An exquisite, almost precious taste was exhibited by the furniture, the pictures and the ornaments. On the wall opposite the fireplace, quite by itself, hung a tapestry recognizable as one of Brass's designs. It was worked in restrained tints of blue, green and yellow, and depicted a formalized group of two nymphs being chased by a faun, the golden-white flesh colours among the big, arbutus-shaped leaves giving the piece a dreamy, ideal character. The books in the case were a small collection of current reading-matter. They suggested a fondness for the more romantic productions of current literature. On a low stand or plinth in a corner stood a piece of modern sculpture, a primitive torso in beech; it had no arms and no legs above the knee, but the vigorous trunk seemed to have a strange, independent life of its own. Gently was still examining it critically when the door opened and Mrs. Page swept fragrantly into the room.

'Oh—Inspector! You wish me to make my statement now?'

She was rather hectically dressed in a leaf-green gown, the swept shoulders of which made Gently shiver.

'You—you will have told Sir Daynes, of course?'

She was trying to be poised and relaxed, but the fund of composure with which she entered the room was forsaking her by leaps and bounds.

'I had lunch with . . . he told me . . . naturally, it was a great relief!'

Only she looked about as relieved as a concert-tuned fiddle.

Gently sighed softly to himself and motioned her to a chair. She felt for it with her hand, her eyes never leaving his face. He closed the door she had left open and stood with his back to it, film-fashion, listening for an instant to the oppressive silence.

'Who else is in this wing besides ourselves and the maid?'

'I—nobody. Nobody at all.'

'I've taken the precaution of bolting the door from the state apartments . . . there'll be an outer door, will there? Do you know if that's unbolted?'

'No . . . I mean, it's bolted. Inspector——'

'You're sure of that?'

'Of course—it's never open!'

'Right. . . . I find it necessary to see to these things.'

He left the door and brought his chair over to the fire, and turned it back-to-front as he had done on the previous occasion.

'Now, Mrs. Page—this time I want it with no holds barred. We've come to the stage where only the truth is good enough—not bits of it, not slants of it, but the whole truth, and damn anybody's feelings! You understand that?'

She nodded at him frightenedly.

'You know what your cousin told me, and you must know what we're thinking. As the facts stand at the moment, I wouldn't be surprised if Sir Daynes arrests him before the day is out.'

'He—he's been behaving . . . very strangely.'

'I'm glad you appreciate that.'

'At lunch, I couldn't understand . . . oh Inspector, I don't know what to think, I don't—I don't!'

'Would you be good enough to describe what passed between you at lunch?'

She clasped her hands together and sat looking at them, lying on her knee. 'He told me . . . what he told you. And after that—I just can't explain it!—he seemed to be saying goodbye. Oh Inspector, it can't be true—you don't believe it—tell me you don't!'

Tears flooded up in the beautiful eyes, and she dabbed at them fiercely with an embroidered handkerchief.

'He told me that I'd be taken care of—that I wasn't to fret about anything that happened. I'd just got to—got to hold my head high—and tell the truth—that was all that mattered. Oh what can I think—what can I believe?'

She couldn't hold the tears back now. They came surging up in great sobs, and soon she was crying helplessly without any effort to restrain it.

'I've known so much of it—so much! I don't want to go on—I'm tired of it—I'm tired of trying. Once it all seemed worthwhile . . . now, I don't want to go on!'

Gently compressed his lips and remained silent, arms crossed over the chair-back. A hideous business—a cruel, pointless business! What ironic power had set this tragic mechanism ticking on a quiet Christmas morning?

'Why couldn't I have done it—why can't you arrest me?'

'I'm sorry, Mrs. Page——'

'It was my fault . . . I should be the one to pay the penalty!'

'I'm afraid the law won't look at it like that.'

Her tears subsided at last. She wiped her reddened eyes with the inadequate rag, and twisted it repeatedly through her clenched fingers. She had a dulled, beaten expression.

'Well . . . what can I possibly tell you?'

Gently made her look at him. 'To begin with, how much did you leave out of what you told me before?'

'I didn't leave anything out.'

'I think you did. I think you must have done.'

'But no—you didn't let me. I told you all, as I promised *him* I would.'

'There's something vital somewhere. . . .'

'Honestly, Inspector—what reason have I got, to lie now?'

There was a ring of conviction about her tear-husky voice, and the eyes faced him squarely. He gave the shadow of a shrug.

'All right—it's something you don't know about! We'll take your statement again, right from the beginning. And think, Mrs. Page, think with all your might and main. Nothing you can say now will injure your cousin very much, but it might very well be that there's a chance somewhere. . . .'

In a low, hopeless voice she began to go over it. Only too plainly, she was convinced that it could do no good. Gently sat crouched like a Buddha, listening, listening, testing each phrase for a new and illuminating connotation.

'When did Earle first pay you attention?'

'On that very first day. . . .'

'What day was that?'

'It was a Thursday, about half-way through November.'

'Who was with you at the time?'

'They were all there . . . it was in the workshop.'

'What else happened that day . . . ?'

Questions he didn't know why he asked, aimless, irrelevant questions. But they kept her mind searching and foraging over the memories of those hours, adding detail to detail, weaving thread after thread into the vague tapestry. . . .

'Is it true that you've never looked at a man since your husband died?'

'Yes . . . quite true.'

'Johnson never made a pass at you?'

'No—of course not!'

'What about the others?'

'There's been nothing like that.'

'Young Wheeler, for instance?'

'No. Certainly not.'

'Brass said he made a pass at you.'

'If he did, I'd forgotten it.'

'Do you know anything of your cousin's plans?'

'No . . . except that he only lives for the workshop.'

'Earle hung around all the women—was he specially interested in the little blonde girl . . . ?'

In the end she seemed to go stupid with the endless probing of the questions. Her answers came automatically, as though he were applying a stimulus to a brain which, without will, was obliged to react to them.

'Wouldn't you have looked round the gallery?'

'No. I wasn't thinking.'

'There were two people on it who both saw you.'

'I didn't see them. I wasn't thinking.'

'What did your cousin say to you about Earle?'

'We didn't discuss him.'

'Who did discuss him?'

'Nobody, in that sense.'

'In what sense, Mrs. Page?'

'In the sense of being interested in me.'

'Did your cousin know you walked out to the folly with him . . . ?'

When he let her do the talking it was very little better. The more she was obliged to dwell on the circumstances, the less hope could she find of her cousin's innocence. And the helpless acceptance of this had something horrible about it. It seemed to destroy some vital principle in her. She sat in the chair, leaning forward and swaying slightly. It would have been a relief now to have seen her burst into tears.

'I want to know *everything* about your relations with Earle!'

'There is nothing to add. I have told you everything.'

'You have told me that you made it publicly clear that you were not interested in him.'

'I can only repeat that. It is entirely true.'

'But you had tête-à-tête with him, Mrs. Page, and they would not be so guarded. Can you truthfully say that nothing passed between you then which a third party might construe as an interest, a deep interest—perhaps *more* than an interest?'

She rocked back, looking at him, the semblance of alertness returning to her lustreless eyes.

'But—but there was no third party. . . .'

'How do you *know* that, Mrs. Page? How do you know you weren't being watched?'

She stared at him, the colour beginning to rise. 'That is ridiculous—I can't believe it, Inspector!'

'But suppose it were true—suppose you were under surveillance—what would that third person have seen, and believed, and perhaps acted upon?'

'No!' she exclaimed, throwing up her hand as though in defence. 'It's too horrible—I can't believe it. He—he would never have done such a thing!'

'But if he did—what would he have seen? That is the crucial point, Mrs. Page! A man has been mur-

dered. Why? What did he do? On the facts we've had
so far, a warning word would have suffced—at the
most, he might have been turned out of the house!
But no—he was murdered—in someone's calendar, he
had committed an unforgivable sin. And you want
me to go on believing it was because he was throwing
himself against the unshakeable rock of your virtue—
just that, and nothing more! The man would have
been laughed at, not killed. He would have been the
jest of the party, not a mark for a murderer's
bludgeon——'

'Stop!' cried Mrs. Page hysterically. 'Stop—I can't
go on listening to you!'

'He was your lover—wasn't he?'

'No—never——'

'Then he was just going to become it.'

'I tell you—Oh stop, stop!'

In a frenzy she threw herself on her knees in front
of him and seized hold of his arms.

'Oh God, if I've done wrong, I'm being punished—
I'm being punished, and I deserve it! But don't go on
saying those things—they aren't true, and perhaps
they never would have been!'

Gently painfully averted his head. 'I'm sorry,' he
said. 'I'm truly sorry, Mrs. Page. But I want the truth,
and I mean to have it . . . if you loved Earle, you
would want it that way.'

She hadn't loved Earle, she persisted, and Gently
believed her. But she had been dangerously and powerfully attracted by him.

'It isn't an easy thing to admit . . . some men
have an impossible fascination for me. I've always

been afraid of myself, even when I was married. I live up to a certain pattern of myself—everyone believes in it—but underneath that I'm sometimes no better than—well, than a whore. My cousin, of course, knows about it. He knows I was nearly sent down from Girton. And though I loved Des so much . . . well, once it happened then too.'

And her husband had died, and she had taken it as a judgment upon herself. From that day onward she had placed an icy barrier between the widowed Mrs. Page and the world of men. To begin with it wasn't difficult. She had been desolated by the loss of her husband. For a time, at least, Somerhayes had been almost her whole acquaintance. When eventually she began to pick up the strings of her life again, she felt confident that she had governed her weakness, and that the lesson she had had was a permanent one. The men she met had no strong attraction for her. It had been easy to repel any advances by her frigid manner and the invocation of her dead husband. Surely and determinedly, she had accepted the permanent status of a faithful widow, and thus she was known to all except Somerhayes.

'I was growing up, you see! When Des died I was only twenty-six, and emotionally, I suppose, a good deal younger than that. But I grew up fast. I learned to keep my balance and to resist temptation. It isn't so terribly difficult, that . . . just an attitude of mind! You can think yourself into anything, and think yourself out again. It's easy to blame the flesh for the indiscipline of the mind. And I had Henry to help me. He was like a devoted brother all the time. At the end of two years, I felt certain I had outgrown the failings of my youth . . . my personality had matured. I was no longer an adolescent.'

Brass had been the big test. He belonged to that class of men whom she had previously found irresistible. He had wasted no time in making a pass at her, and here she had lacked the support of Somerhayes, who, being an idolatrous admirer of Brass, had more or less passed his blessing on the connexion. But her hardly-won virtue had shakily triumphed. Brass was resisted, and bearing no malice, had settled down comfortably to the role of friendship. Lovemaking, after all, was a somewhat marginal detail as far as the artist was concerned. . . .

'Did he know he had this attraction for you?' pondered Gently.

'Oh yes, I'm sure he did—there isn't much you can hide from Les! But he saw I didn't want it, and that was enough. Les is very genuine, you know, once you see through his artistic flummery. Ever since then we've been on the best of terms.'

Confirmed by this victory, and with the addition of Brass to her trusted intimacy, she felt assured of her new measurement with life. The invitation to Merely had come just at the right time. She had begun to be bored by her comparatively inactive existence in Chelsea. The association with Somerhayes and Brass, the two people most respected by her, coupled to an existing new venture in which she could develop her latent ability for business, was exactly what she required to satisfy her desire to be doing something. She had thrown all her enthusiasm and industry into the establishment of the workshop. She had conducted a market-analysis, opened relationships with the large furnishing and interior decorating firms, fought a one-woman war to convince buyers that tapestry was really worth an economic price, arranged an exhibition, and secured widespread press notices. The past eighteen months had been a delirious whirl of activity. There had been no time to brood over personal relations. The venture was succeeding, the market was beginning to open out, a second section of the out-buildings was already being adapted for another six looms.

'And then . . . Earle came along.'

Immediately, she had heard the warning bell ring in her darkest being. Earle was everything that spelt temptation, and what was more, he knew it. Just as she recognized him, he recognized her, and in spite of her diffidence he could see success beckoning to him in her eyes. And to him, it was more important than it was to Brass. To him, young, callow, inexperienced and unsure of himself, it was a driving force that recognized no obstacle or scruple. From the moment of their introduction he was determined to possess her. He didn't know quite how to do it, but do it he would. Instinctively cunning, he realized that she would permit no direct approach, and instead he substituted his bantering, exaggerated gallantry which it was impossible for her to do other than accept with a good grace. But underneath it had been the fire, and both of them had known it. And Somerhayes, of course, had known it too.

'I don't have to tell you how important that is. . . .'

She nodded. 'I know . . . but you'll guess it if I

don't tell you. And he told me to tell the truth . . .
though I'm not holding my head very high.'

He had shown that he knew in a thousand little
ways. Wasn't he an expert, now, at keeping an eye on
his cousin? He had said nothing to her directly. On
this subject he had never been notably articulate. But
she had taken his look, his hesitation, his inflection as
certainly as she would have done a speech from another person. Don't let yourself go—that had been the
message. He knew she was in danger, but she mustn't
let herself go. And in public she had obeyed him. She
had kept Earle dancing at a distance. As far as the
world went, he was the court jester, with a licence.

'Didn't Brass tumble to it?'

'No—that's where Earle showed himself particularly
clever. He realized that Les was very sharp-sighted,
and he went out of his way to pull the wool over his
eyes. I'm not saying that Earle wasn't interested in
tapestry—he had a genuine flair for it, not to mention
a business instinct. But he wasn't as keen as he made
Les believe. At least half of it was laid on for Les's
special benefit. And it worked as it was bound to.
Tapestry, for Les, is the dominating factor in life,
and if you keep him buttered-up with it he's quite
blind to anything else going on round him. At the
same time Earle was paying court to the other three
women in the shop, as though it was just his way. He
had a cunning that was almost devilish, and only my
cousin and myself could appreciate it.'

While they were with the others the charade was
played out, but once they were alone together Earle
dropped his mask.

'It was this two-facedness of his that helped me to

resist him, I think. In spite of his charm one could feel an element of calculation about him, a cold, egoistic weighing of the chances. He knew I was attracted to him physically, and he used it against me like a weapon, like a—yes!—like a bludgeon. By that he was to stop my objections, to wear me down. Any demur of mine was to be met by an embrace and passionate kisses. But he was overplaying his hand, and I didn't quite fall for it. Always there was that feeling of being manipulated like an animal. I was on the verge of giving in to him, it seems miraculous that I didn't; and if I did not, it was due to his mistaken judgment rather than to my virtue. If he had tried a little less, he might have got everything.'

'But there were . . . intimacies . . . passing between you?'

'Yes. I have admitted it.'

'Enough to have suggested a certain conclusion?'

'If anyone had seen them . . . please, don't make me think of that!'

On Christmas Eve there was a sense of crisis between them. She had refused to go on that 'shopping' expedition with him, and his reaction to her refusal had shown her how much she had wounded him. He came back to find her in a relenting mood, and immediately sought to take advantage of it. There had been a passionate interlude in the folly, followed by a shorter passage in the ante-room to her wing. Now he was in the house it was obvious that he intended to press his suit to the utmost. The assignation she had been expecting, and accepted with a resignation that was very near to consent; but when it actually took place, she had re-experienced that feeling of revulsion towards him, and had broken away and fled to the sanctuary of her wing.

'And he didn't follow you—you've nothing to add to that part?'

'No—I gave you the facts. I think he was staggered at my running away. You see, I didn't say anything at all—I just felt I couldn't stand it any longer, and slipped loose and dashed out. A moment before he must have been congratulating himself on at last having got his way.'

Gently gazed dully at the floor. 'Plenty enough there for jealousy!' he mused.

She looked up at him wonderingly. 'Jealousy . . . ? Why do you say that?'

'Why?' He shrugged. 'I'm afraid there's not much doubt about that!'

'But my cousin wouldn't be jealous.'

'Mmn?' It was his turn to look up.

'No—that's quite absurd! He—he's never given any indication. Do you think for one moment——' She broke off in something like confusion. 'It's ridiculous, I tell you! You don't know anything about Henry. He wants me to marry Les—that's the whole text of his sermon.'

'I know about that——'

'Then you know about everything. Henry isn't jealous of me—he's jealous for Les. It's been his idea that I should marry Les ever since—oh, I don't know when! But if you think that he has the remotest interest in me personally, I can soon tell you that you're mistaken.'

'Are you sure of that, Mrs. Page . . . ?'

'Sure? Oh God! If you were me, you would be sure, Inspector.'

'He just wants you to marry Brass?'

'Yes. Yes, that's all he wants!'

'Badly enough to have done . . . what he may have done?'

'Yes . . . to have done it three times over!'

She was crying again now, not tempestuously but with a heart-rending bitterness, crying with wide-open eyes over which the tears flooded before falling.

'You see—I made a mess of it for everyone—everyone who had to do with me! My husband—he's dead. Earle . . . he loved me. And now, because of that, Henry—Henry too! There's a curse on this family. We did wrong, we are being punished. It will be best when there are no more Feverells on the face of the earth. . . .'

Very quietly Gently rose and replaced his chair where it belonged.

'Where did your cousin say I'd find him, Mrs. Page?' he enquired.

'He said he'd be in the hall—he said he'd be waiting for you there!'

Gently nodded and took his hat. 'I won't keep him waiting any longer. Your cousin, Mrs. Page, has a wonderful sense of theatre.'

CHAPTER FOURTEEN

OUTSIDE IT was dusk, and in the great hall more than dusk; when Gently entered by the north-east door to the gallery, he noticed with an ironical hunch of a shoulder that only the night-light by the main door had been switched on. But of course, he had to understand everything! In a case like this mere facts were the province of the Sir Dayneses and the Dysons. He, Gently, was required to relive the crime, he was the selected repository for the spiritual remains of the last of the Feverells . . . and wasn't he playing the game, making his entry where Somerhayes had made it on the night of the drama? Wasn't he pat on cue for the final, majestic scene?

He stopped behind the first pillar, nearly opposite to the door. Yes, this undoubtedly would be where Somerhayes had taken his stand. From here you could see without being seen. You would have been out of sight of Johnson, coming in by the south-east door. You would have escaped a glance from Mrs. Page, crossing and recrossing the landing between the marble portal and the north-west door. But you, you could see everything. The hall, the stairs, the landing, the galleries, they were all overlooked from this lurk-

ing-place. You could, for instance, have seen Lieutenant Earle, if he had been standing in the precise
centre of the top stair, where Somerhayes was standing now. . . .

'Quite right, Mr. Gently!'

The sixth Baron's voice came softly to him down
the hall, a sort of mocking commentary to his
thoughts.

'Actually, I stood a little nearer to the pillar, but
not enough to make a significant difference.'

Gently grunted and made the adjustment. He
wasn't above taking stage-directions! Now, he could
see rather less of the hall below, but a good deal
more of the landing ahead. Without hurrying himself, he went over every detail of the view thus
presented.

'That pillar there, flanking the portico——'

'Yes, Mr. Gently?'

'The one on the left-hand side . . . would you
mind standing beside it for a minute?'

Somerhayes didn't move to it directly. He seemed
to be pondering over the direction. But eventually,
with what may have been a shrug, he turned from the
stairs and pressed himself in beside the pillar.

'Now just stay there, will you?'

Gently plodded down to the landing, and having
reached it, stood for some minutes with his back to
the north-west door. Then he crossed the landing, ne-
gotiated the south gallery, and spent a similar period
at the spot where Johnson had emerged. Somerhayes
watched these manœuvres without a word.

'All right—that's everything!' Gently returned to
the landing, hands in pockets. 'Personally, I'd sooner

talk by that library fire of yours, but I wouldn't want to spoil a good production over a trifle like that. Whose cue is it—yours or mine?'

'Yours, Mr. Gently.' Somerhayes sounded a little piqued.

'Good—because I've got a lot to say—and I hope I've understood this business the way you wanted me to!'

Somerhayes made a frigid motion with his head and took up his position at the top of the stairs again. Gently, huddled in his ulster, paced up and down the twilit landing behind him.

'In the first place it wasn't a crime of passion—that's what I'm supposed to know, isn't it?'

Somerhayes said nothing, but stood looking out into the hall beneath.

'It looks like that, and that may be the case for the prosecution—but between you and me, it's something quite different! Because you don't love your cousin in a possessive way, do you? It's brotherly love, a kinsman's love, a love that wants to see her married, not to a decadent aristocrat, but to one of the world's creators—a man, shall we say, strong in the flow of history. She's the last possible flame of the torch of Feverell. You want to attach her, and the Feverell blood, to an aristocrat of the new world succeeding your own. And by doing that, you want to serve this man, you want to ensure his future and the success of his genius.

'Prompt me where I go wrong—you know the picture better than I do!'

Somerhayes didn't move. 'I was sure,' he murmured, 'I was sure I could depend on you, Mr. Gently. . . .'

'All this you had planned when you walked out of the House of Lords. That was the old world, the Lords, the old world of privilege and greed and suppression and social injustice. Oh, it had its leavening of progressives, its top-dressing of Socialism; but you had looked deeper, hadn't you? You had seen its essential corruption. You saw it as an old soldier with a historic death-rattle in its throat, and you knew, though it could still wave its sword and utter threats, that it was doomed as surely as jingoism and the satanic mills! So you turned your back, and left the dead to bury the dead. You took your courage in both hands, you faced the situation of being of a tainted race, and you applied your energy, money and affection to the service of a prophet of the new world—Leslie Brass.

'Out of your ruins, he could rise. From your extinction, his erection. Though you had come into this life ignobly in the eyes of history, yet in those same eyes you would leave it truly ennobled! Am I right so far? Have I got the authentic text?'

'Yes!' breathed Somerhayes. 'You have the authentic text!'

'There was only one flaw in the plan—your cousin and Brass were unattached romantically. Mrs. Page, for various reasons, was still guarding herself from contact with men, and Brass, though he may amuse himself with women, was apparently not in the market for a wife. Yet it was critically necessary for these two to come together. You would have done your duty to neither by simply splitting the inheritance between

them. Brass, to succeed, needed Mrs. Page's management—and she needed him to provide a sheet-anchor!
So you tried to help the matter on. You willed your
estate to your cousin. Brass, cognisant of this, was supposed to open his campaign.

'That was how the matter stood when Earle came
into the reckoning. You had put your last card on the
table, and you were waiting for game to be called.
The affair stood at its crisis. You could afford no in-
tervention. And then, out of the sheer perversity of
fate, Earle appeared with his single trump-card!

'What could you do? What could you possibly do?
Nothing, except watch, and perhaps pray that your
cousin would resist the young man. And she tried to
resist him. She put up a struggle. And you watched,
and waited, and pretended to see nothing.'

Gently paused in his stride to look at the slender
figure silhouetted against the dimly-lit hall.

'At what point did you decide to kill him?'

'I don't know.' Somerhayes's voice was almost too
low to catch.

'Was it when you invited him here to spend Christmas?'

'It might have been then. That might have been
my idea.'

'Well, we'll leave it to the prosecution—they'll love
fighting that out!' Gently stalked on, fists stuck out
like rods in his pockets. 'But the idea came to you—
and it was a fascinating one too. It was nothing as
simple as merely getting rid of Earle. If that had been
all, you might not have done it. Or you might have
done it more cleverly—a gun accident, for instance!
But Earle was more than an obstacle. He was also a

means to an end. As you contemplated the act you saw all its consequences—you saw the disposition of fate as clearly as though you had it in writing. *Here* was the great Finis, the end you would have sought for yourself—here was the ultimate challenge to stamp your life with significance! Symbolically you would be the sacrifice, the old to the new. With your life, at one stroke, you could repay the debt of your family to society. And in addition to that you would die a martyr—the abolitionist would die by the hand of the hangman. And from the dock, the guilty dock, your voice would be heard. You could thunder to the four quarters of the earth the speech which fell stillborn in the House of Betrayal!

'Am I still quoting the text? Have you nothing to add?'

'Go on!' panted Somerhayes. 'Go on to the end!'

'So we come to that particular night, when you overheard the assignation. It was near one in the morning, with everyone in bed or about to retire there. The need and the opportunity had come together. The fate you felt so strongly had provided the moment. You crept after Earle. You were not standing down there by the north-east door. Here is where you were crouching, here beside this pillar, beside the portico, beneath the panel with the truncheons—where your cousin couldn't see you, nor, as it happened, could Johnson either! And you saw your cousin come, you heard the interview that took place, you saw Johnson come out to look, you saw your cousin return to her wing. And then you saw Earle leave the saloon—stand where you are standing now!—you plucked that truncheon from its panel, and you struck him down the stairs.

'Why did you wipe the truncheon? Perhaps you can fill in that little item! It could be that you wanted the sensation of the slow approach of justice. In any case, you made certain that it would find you. You phoned the County Constabulary before you phoned Sir Daynes. Sir Daynes, as you knew, would try to find for accidental death, but once you'd given Dyson a smell of the scent, he'd follow you to the kill! Only it so happened that I was around too, and I was given the preference . . . while Sir Daynes was sidetracked by Johnson, you carefully kept me pointing in the right direction.'

Gently stopped opposite the gasping nobleman.

'And that's that, my lord—everything I should know!'

'Take me!' exclaimed Somerhayes, twisting round with outstretched hands. 'I want you to make the arrest—I want you to do it—personally!'

Gently stood looking at him for a long, pitiless moment. Then he slowly shook his head.

'No,' he said. 'It's too fantastic . . . it's psychologically impossible!'

'You must arrest me—I demand it!'

Somerhayes was still holding out his hands. And Gently was still shaking his head with obstinate decision.

'I knew you were to be the man—I appeal to you to do it!'

'*I* may be the man'—Gently shrugged—'but *you're* not the man . . . there's the contradiction!'

'Mr. Gently, you have grasped the whole case. As a magistrate, I adjure you to do your duty——!'

'I am trying to grasp it, my lord, and I shall certainly do my duty. But I repeat . . . you are not the man to commit a crime like this. You are a man to die—yes! But you are not a man to kill. Your whole record makes nonsense of the account I have just drawn up.'

'How dare you make such a judgment!'

'I dare, from the facts you have given me.'

'In so many words, Mr. Gently, I hereby confess to the murder of Lieutenant Earle!'

'I'm sorry, my lord, but your character prevents me from accepting your word in the matter.'

Somerhayes's hands fell to his sides, and he seemed to shrink back insensibly from the sudden, dramatic pose he had assumed. In the dim light it was impossible to distinguish the expression of his features or his eyes. He was merely a black-etched shape against the impoverished illumination below.

'Mr. Gently, I beseech you'—his voice had sunk again to its lowest tone—'I beseech you to think well what you are doing before you take an irrevocable step. I can count on your understanding. I can count on yours alone. Do not press too far for the ultimate fact, when it may not be in the service of the ultimate truth. Consider, Mr. Gently—I beseech you to consider!'

'Mmn.' Gently stood planted like a brooding statue.

'Think again what manner of man I am. Be fearless, be favourless in your summing-up. You know I see myself truly. I am a spiritual man of straw, a decadent, an anachronism, one without value. My only

good is to die well, my only excuse to have served an
ideal. Before you interrupt what is wholly the course
of justice, think—think!'

Gently nodded from his shadowy silence.

'If men have purpose, and I believe they have, then
the worthless have value when they accept the dis-
positions of providence. And this disposition is mine.
By this I fulfil what would appear a useless destiny.
Have you the right to withhold your assistance from
me at this moment, or to tamper with a disposal bearing the stamp of higher purpose? I say you have not,
Mr. Gently, and I insist that you acknowledge it!'

Gently hunched his shapeless shoulders, looked
away, and looked back again.

'You can die, my lord,' he said, 'but you can't kill.
That's all I acknowledge just now! And if you didn't
kill Lieutenant Earle, then you are proposing to die
for another—and who else can that other be but
Leslie Edward Brass?'

'No!' cried Somerhayes. 'Be reasonable, Mr.
Gently!'

'Brass,' repeated Gently, his voice beginning to rise.
'I say again—who else, my lord? Who else but the
man you would turn into an idol? You have sacrificed
your career to him—your money—your cousin's love.
And now you want to make the great sacrifice—don't
you?—to lay down your life!'

'I am nothing!' exclaimed Somerhayes. 'Remember—I am nothing.'

'On the contrary,' snapped Gently. 'You are the
most profound egotist I have ever had to deal with!'

The nobleman reeled as though he had been struck
in the face. The half-light below, catching him in

profile, showed the white of his eye in a shocked dilation.

'You shouldn't have said that!' he stammered. 'Mr. Gently, you shouldn't have said it!'

'No, I shouldn't—should I?' demanded Gently. 'It wasn't in the compact! My business was to stop short where you were still a heroic figure. Unfortunately I am not a hero-worshipper, my lord. You mistook your man when you cast me for the part. In the course of a long connexion with the criminal character, I've been driven to the conclusion that the biggest heroes are the greatest criminals—they are psychopaths, my lord, people who have failed, like you, to reach a working compromise with life.'

Somerhayes caught hold of the balustrade and hung to it, gasping. 'You are killing me!' he cried. 'Every word is like a dagger!'

'The truth won't kill!' Gently pressed on mercilessly. 'You're going to face it this time, unlike all the other occasions, when you only played at facing it. Because you never have faced it yet, have you? From Jepson down to the House of Lords and Janice it's been one long retreat—a retreat to preserve the myth—a retreat to keep intact the vision of Lord Somerhayes the Great. *This* is what I've come to understand. *This* is where the focus starts getting sharp. You care nothing for your cousin. You care nothing for society. To keep the myth unblemished you would sacrifice the love of the one and bequeath the other a killer—and step on the scaffold in an intoxication of self-love and imaginary grandeur. Where is the hero here, my lord? Where is the nobility I have been summoned to admire? All I can see is a gigantic selfishness, and an egotism so voracious that only tragedy can glut it!'

'I have served art!' cried Somerhayes. 'Give me that at least—creation absolves the greatest of crimes!'

'You serve yourself,' retorted Gently. 'You have never served anything else. And as for crime, it has no absolution but punishment.'

'Personally,' said a third voice behind them, 'I prefer his lordship's version, Inspector!' And Leslie Brass stepped suddenly out of the unlit saloon.

'Keep your voices down, children . . . I'm getting to be somewhat *de trop* around here.'

Brass had a gun in his hand, a small automatic which Gently recognized as a .22 Unique of French manufacture.

'I don't want to raise my bag unnecessarily, but you see how I'm placed, my chickens. As I take it, his lordship is just about to rat on me—you used the right weapon, Inspector. Flattery would have got you nowhere!'

Gently shrugged expressionlessly. 'I was wondering when you'd come out. . . .'

'Of course you were, my son.' Brass waved the gun deprecatingly. 'It's your business to notice things, isn't it? If X was listening-in on two consecutive occasions, the odds are pretty bright that he would be there the third time. And here he is, toying with his lordship's gun . . . what does that suggest to the trained police mind?'

'You'd never get away with it.'

'I might, you know, all things considered.'

'At the moment, Brass, you could get off with manslaughter . . . it'll be a different tale if you fool around with that thing.'

'You visualize the whole plot I take it, my maestro?'

'You're thinking you could shoot the pair of us and leave the gun in his lordship's hand.'

'Distinctly workable, y'know.'

'The police aren't fools.'

'But they're thinking along certain lines, Inspector. They would rush to jump at the wrong conclusion. What could be more natural than for his lordship, being taxed, to draw his gun and shoot you—and then to put an end to things? There's only my conscience really to worry about . . . and it's a pretty elastic article. The first job is the worst, sonny. After that it gets to be routine.'

Gently grunted and turned to Somerhayes. 'You see?' he said. 'You see what you're protecting? This is crime, not creation. Art doesn't kill, but greed does.'

Brass gave his cynical laugh. 'Too true, professor, too true. I thought you might have been harbouring the idea that I killed Earle for Janice. . . . I did, of course, but only in an incidental way. It's filthy lucre that makes the world go round.'

'Don't say that!' gasped Somerhayes, still supporting himself by the balustrade. 'I won't hear it from you—it's nothing but your way of talking.'

'And as I talk I am—just get that into your befuddled brain!'

'The spirit is there . . . you cannot blaspheme the spirit!'

'The spirit my backside—I killed him for the cash!'

Gently never had a chance to stop it. Without warning Somerhayes came flying off the balustrade

like a galvanized frog. The inevitable had to happen.
He went spinning sideways to the crash and blaze of
the gun. At the same second Gently hurled himself
on the artist and sent the gun flying over the
rail. . . .

'Traitor!' cried Somerhayes, clutching his bloody
shoulder on the floor. 'You should have killed me—
why didn't you kill me?'

'I would have done, you stupid bastard!' shouted
Brass, dodging Gently. 'Take it as an omen—your
number was on that bullet!'

He dived through the north-west door, slamming it
in Gently's face. When the Central Office man got it
open it was to see the door to the staircase slamming
a few yards ahead. He burst it open with his shoulder. Brass was tearing up the spiral stairs. A couple of
turns behind, Gently panted up after him.

'Come back!' he bawled. 'You're cornered, Brass.
You'll never get off the roof!'

The artist wasted no breath in reply, but continued
his flight down the attic corridors.

Along there it was black as the inside of a hat.
Gently could hear his quarry stumbling and bumping
up ahead as he plunged after him, similarly handi-
capped. The door to the hatch slammed, and then
the door of the hatch itself. Out in the whining gale
that cut over the leads he could just make out Brass
sliding and slipping towards the south-east wing. At
the angle he must get him—there was no way back
from there! But then, at the angle, Brass went over
the coping like a monkey, and when he got to it
Gently found a fire-ladder leading down to the wing-
roof below. He went down the ladder. Brass was al-

ready on the far side of the wing. Another ladder took them down to the coach-house roof, and then another one to the garage-yard. . . .

Outdistanced, Gently came to the last ladder just as Brass was reaching the bottom. With a mental prayer he lowered himself over, hung poised, and let himself go. . . . He got Brass all right. He bowled him over like a nine-pin. But unfortunately he got himself as well, and it was some few moments before his wind came back and he was able to renew an intelligent interest in events.

When at last he was able to scramble to his feet, a dazzling beam of light stabbed at him and made him throw up his arm defensively.

'Waal, waal!' exclaimed a well-remembered voice. 'If it isn't the Chief Inspector doing gymnastics off the roof! And who is this other athlete, Inspector—would he be somebody who I ought to know?'

The torch beam lowered and reversed. It revealed Colonel Rynacker, U.S.A.F. It also revealed a couple of Snowdrops supporting a sick-looking Brass, a Brass who had patently had most of the bounce knocked out of him.

'Guess I brought these boys along to give a hand to your cops . . . when we ran across this guy he seemed to think we were hostile. But what goes, Chief Inspector? How come the schemozzle?'

Gently grimaced and felt himself over tenderly. 'It's nothing,' he said. 'It's just my night for these things. . . .'

CHAPTER FIFTEEN

BRASS MADE his statement, and a very clever one it was, too. Its sheer, reckless audacity compelled admiration for the man. Undeterred by Gently in his window seat, or Somerhayes, pale from the loss of blood and with his arm in a sling, the artist rolled off a story which either one of them could have punctured in a dozen places. And all the while his green eyes twinkled ironically from one to the other. . . .

He was returning to the north-east wing to fetch his lighter, that was the tale. On entering the great hall by the south-west door to the gallery, he had heard the voices of Mrs. Page and Earle raised in the saloon. Naturally, he had been unable to avoid overhearing what was being said, and the purport of it had made him hesitate by the door in case Mrs. Page needed assistance. In the event, Mrs. Page succeeded in breaking away from Earle. With the final injunction to him that he had better leave in the morning, she had hastily departed in the direction of her own apartment. For some moments Earle had remained in the saloon, and Brass was about to pass on under the impression that the American had given up his intentions. Before he could do so, however, Earle rushed out of the saloon in obvious pursuit of Mrs. Page, and Brass had siezed his arm and attempted to re- monstrate with him. The American had refused to lis- ten. He had grappled with Brass and attempted to throw him down. In the course of the struggle Brass was hurled against the wall under the panel of truncheons, and as Earle turned to continue his pur- suit of Mrs. Page, Brass had seized one of the truncheons and struck the American on the back of the head.

It went without saying that the blow was not in- tended to be fatal. Brass's sole object had been to dis- able Earle and to prevent him carrying out what appeared to be a criminal purpose. Unfortunately he had struck not wisely but too well, and Earle, after tottering a few steps, had toppled lifelessly down the great stairs. Brass, shocked and alarmed at the result of what he had done, but realizing that it would probably pass as an accidental fall, had wiped and re- placed the truncheon and left the affair to develop as it might. He had not been apprehensive when suspi- cion fell on Johnson, since he felt that the police were proceeding on grounds palpably insufficient (here he was obliged to pause while Sir Daynes baronetized once or twice), but in a recent interview with his lordship and Chief Inspector Gently it had been represented to him that his lordship was now under suspicion; he therefore felt it incumbent on him to confess. He realized that he had done wrongly in attempting concealment. He deeply regretted the trouble and unpleasantness it had caused. If any part of his statement were not quite clear, he would be happy to supply every detail that might assist complete clarification.

Sir Daynes was openly baffled by this masterly blueprint for a verdict of manslaughter. He scratched his grizzled locks and fired a number of his most telling glances at the apparently contrite artist. Things had happened which didn't seem to have got on the record—odd, preposterous and downright unofficial things! The baronet had the feeling that he was being left out somewhere, and nobody seemed to be rushing to put him in the picture. . . .

'All right,' he said at last. 'Dyson, charge this feller with manslaughter. I'll get on to you later if there's to be any amendment of the charge. Oh, and regarding that other feller, Johnson——'

'Yes sir?' enquired Dyson bleakly.

'Better drop the charge, man—sort of thing doesn't do our reputation any good!'

Dyson departed looking as though Christmas hadn't done much for him, with him his supporters and the handcuffed Brass. Sir Daynes slewed in his chair to confront his lordship and Gently. Colonel Rynacker, who had been a silent witness to the processes of the goddamned, also appeared to have items on his mind.

'Well?' demanded Sir Daynes, raking the Somerhayes-Gently sector. 'You're not going to tell me it's as simple as all that, eh? Got a spoke, haven't you, to put in that feller's wheel?'

Somerhayes nursed his bandaged shoulder and glanced across at Gently. It was an appealing, part-reproachful, part-admonishing look, and the Central Office man replied with the merest inflexion of his

shoulders. Somerhayes nodded back an acknowledgement which was equally discrete.

'I do not think there is a great deal to add, Sir
Daynes,' he said in his flat-toned way of speaking. 'I
am prepared to amend my statement, of course, to
confirm the fact that Brass was present in the hall. . . .'

'Yes, yes—don't doubt it, don't doubt it!' interrupted Sir Daynes impatiently. 'But what about this—
hah—interview that's supposed to have taken place
between Gently and you and Brass—bit more than an
interview, wasn't it, judging by results?'

'It served its purpose, Sir Daynes . . . I doubt
whether it is necessary to encumber your case with
the particular details.'

'Not even though you got winged, man, and Gently
had to chase Brass over the tiles?'

Somerhayes squirmed a little and glanced at Gently
again. The Chief Inspector was sitting hunched like
an owl in a belfry, an expression of extraordinary
blankness on his face.

'There were factors of this interview, Sir Daynes,
which, as a magistrate, I have naturally been obliged
to consider with great care. It was a consultation in
which, admittedly, a great deal of emotion was involved. Rash words were spoken in anger, foolish de-
terminations evoked and acted upon. But I believe
that the only certain and significant thing to emerge
from it is Mr. Brass's willingness to confess, and that
the admission as evidence of what preceded it can
only be prejudicial to the proper end of justice. You
must therefore excuse me from being more explicit.'

'But damn it all, man!' exploded Sir Daynes with
warmth. 'If that's your attitude, what sort of case

have we got against this feller, eh? Next thing we
know he'll be getting off clean, with the confounded
judge patting him on the back for doing his civic
duty!'

Somerhayes smiled thinly and made his little bow.
'I'm sorry,' he said, 'but I am obliged to act according
to my conscience, Sir Daynes.'

'And you, Gently!' barked Sir Daynes, turning on
the Central Office man. 'I suppose you're backing
Somerhayes up—won't breathe a word about this afternoon?'

Gently stirred in his window seat. 'It's not for me
to argue with a magistrate,' he replied.

Sir Daynes gazed at them nonplussed. Never before
had he met such a plain case of obstruction, with so
little that could be legitimately done about it. If they
wouldn't come clean they wouldn't—and there was
nothing he could confounded-well do to make them!
He had got his man, he had got his confession, and
what more could a Chief Constable reasonably ask for?

'At the same time. . . .' mused Gently.

'Eh?' snapped Sir Daynes.

'According to *my* conscience, you'd better make
that charge murder . . . with manslaughter, of
course, as the happy alternative.'

'No!' exclaimed Somerhayes, rising to his feet. 'As a
magistrate, Mr. Gently——'

Gently stopped him with a gesture.

'As a magistrate, my lord, you can appreciate my
point. You can appreciate the importance of your
will as prosecution evidence. It gave Brass a murderer's motive. He should be compelled to explain
that motive. My conscience doesn't think that the

shadow of the gallows will be a bad thing for Mr. Brass. . . .'

Somerhayes sank back trembling, what colour he had had drained out of his handsome cheeks.

'Perhaps you are right, Mr. Gently,' he murmured. 'Perhaps you are right. . . . I will inform Sir Daynes of the circumstances of the will.'

Gently nodded his mandarin nod. 'I think that's best. Especially as Mr. Brass is such an admirable explainer. . . .'

The charge was duly amended to murder and the alternative. Sir Daynes, if not happy, was satisfied with the case he was turning in. The feller might get off, in fact it was on the cards that he would, but a brush with the black cap followed by a few years segregation would make him think deeply before breaking out again. And, in the meantime, Somerhayes was clear. The son of his old friend was not to be exhibited in the dock at the next Quarter Sessions. By and large, things could have been a lot worse . . . and damnation! It was still Christmas, however irregularly the season had started off.

'I guess the Lieutenant stuck his neck out,' admitted the Colonel over a friendly Scotch. 'If these youngsters will go skirt-hunting in other people's preserves, then jeez, they're asking for it, and you can quote Dwight P. Rynacker as saying so. You know something, Bart?'

'No,' replied Sir Daynes innocently. 'I don't know anything.'

'I been holding out on you, Bart, I been keeping back Earle's dossier. I had it here this morning, right in my brief-case, only when you got so goddam rum-bumptious I reckoned you could darned-well carry on without it.'

Sir Daynes glanced at him indignantly. '*Me* get goddam rumbumptious?' he echoed.

'Waal'—the Colonel grinned at him out of his jowls—'someone got goddam rumbumptious, and I guess that dossier stayed right in my brief-case. But I got it here again now, and you can have a go-over. The Lootenant wasn't quite the blue-eyed boy he gave out, Bart. He'd been in skirt-trouble before, here and back home. One time I cracked down on his leave this Christmas, when I found out where he was spending it, but I guess I didn't like to be hard at this time of the year, and after a man-to-man talk about the facts of life I gave him his pass back. Which just goes to show, don't it? Ain't no goddam use being a sentimental Colonel!'

'Feller took me in,' growled Sir Daynes to his whisky. 'Damned impertinent and that, but I couldn't help liking him.'

'Heck, everyone *liked* him,' assented the Colonel. 'That's just where the catch lay, Bart. He'd got a charm index about ninety-five at proof. But the old Adam was tucked away there, don't you forget it, and all the more dangerous on account of being hid up.'

Gently sat smoking an American cigar and contrib-uting nothing to the conversation. He'd been taken in too . . . if that was how you'd describe it! He could see Earle now, unwrapping his presents on the seat of that first-class compartment. He could hear the young airman's voice with its thrill of enthusiasm and expectation. So there'd been a flaw in that fresh young character, a streak of cold selfishness, perhaps, among the layers of friendly warmth. Was he different in that from the rest of humanity? Was he particularly damned for being imperfect?—One took the good with the bad, the rough with the smooth. In the compound of mortality none dared to require perfection. Yet Earle's weakness had been fatal to him. Out of a thousand chances he had drawn the intolerant one. A cooler, more forbidding, less generous man might never have attracted retribution for his failings, nor ever have gladdened a single soul. Who had Earle taken in? Who had expected him to be a god?

'Guess I'll miss him,' said the Colonel. 'Guess I'll miss the young hound! He got drafted over here at the same time as me. Came in the same flight, we did, way back in August. Reckon we'll fly him back, too . . . his folk'll expect that.'

'Hmph! Inquest to-morrow,' said Sir Daynes gruffly.

'Yeah . . . I know the ropes. I'll have a waggon there to collect him.'

The fire burned red, and Sir Daynes, coming out of a revery with a jerk, suddenly remembered that his spouse was keeping a lonely vigil in the Manor House.

'Hah—Gently'! he exclaimed. 'Better be getting back, man . . . there's nothing we can do here, and Somerhayes has gone off to jaw things over with his cousin. Care to join us over at my place, Colonel? I can guarantee the central heating!'

The Colonel nodded, getting to his feet. 'I'd surely appreciate that, Bart, right now.'

'It'll be a change of blasted atmosphere—I try to

keep business out of the home. Outside it, y'know, I'm the Chief Constable of Northshire, but once I cross that confounded threshold I'm just Gwendoline's husband. . . .'

Lady Broke had her skating, and, by way of a special and not-to-be-adopted-as-precedent dispensation, Gently was indulged in another day's pike-fishing, by means of an air-hole cut in the ice. This proved to be a highly successful operation. The pike, wholly innocent of the dangers of air-holes, almost hung around waiting for the gleam of Gently's spoon. Certainly, he didn't get a specimen. The largest, an eighteen-pounder, was no rival for the celebrated heavy-weight that graced the wall in Finchley. But they bit firm and they bit often, and the average weight was gratifyingly high. At the dusky end of the day Gently struck his gear with the complacent feeling of a man who had really been among the pike, and having been there, had acquitted himself. A snapshot taken by Sir Daynes provided a permanent record of the fact.

Of Somerhayes Gently saw no more before he returned to town. He did not attend the inquest, which dealt merely with identification, and Sir Daynes, who did, reported that Somerhayes 'hadn't got a blasted word for him, not for anyone else as far as he could see.'

'Poor man,' commented Lady Broke, whose maternal interest in Somerhayes never flagged. 'It's been a shocking time for him, Daynes, truly shocking. I shudder to think of what he must have been through. If I were him I would take a long, long holiday in—you know, the West Indies or somewhere like that. And I would take Janice Page with me. I think it's ridiculous, how he doesn't marry her!'

Sir Daynes pooh-poohed, but his prescient lady maintained her opinion; and whether the idea was communicated to Somerhayes supersensorily or by more material media, he did, in fact, very shortly depart with Janice for the sunny shores of Jamaica. Johnson, who proved quite capable of the task, was left to manage the tapestry workshop.

'I *liked* the Inspector,' said Gertrude Winfarthing dreamily, as, with the housemaid, she stripped the now-vacant bed. 'Give me a ten-bob note he did, which is more than half of them do. An' he got a *twinkle* in his eye . . . did you notice his twinkle, Irene? I reckon a girl like me could do worse than marry a man like that, spite of his being fiftyish and always got a pipe in his mouth. . . .'

And she kept her piece of mistletoe for quite a long time afterwards.